The Mongo Mysteries

SHADOW OF A BROKEN MAN

CITY OF WHISPERING STONE

AN AFFAIR OF SORCERERS

THE BEASTS OF VALHALLA

TWO SONGS THIS ARCHANGEL SINGS

CITY
OF
WHISPERING
STONE

BY

George C. Chesbro

A DELL BOOK

Published by
Dell Publishing Co., Inc.
1 Dag Hammarskjold Plaza
New York, New York 10017

Dell ® TM 681510, Dell Publishing Co., Inc.

ISBN: 0-440-20035-0

Reprinted by arrangement with the author

Printed in the United States of America

January 1988

10 9 8 7 6 5 4 3 2 1

KRI

Again for Ori, who loves the land so much.
And for Mark.

I

NEW YORK

1

My ex-boss looked uncomfortable and out of place on the campus—an unkempt genie who'd popped without warning from the bottle of my past. Dressed in baggy pants and an ancient, patched sweater, Phil Statler was a jagged memory of my former world waiting for me on the sidewalk.

That memory loosed a swarm of others which buzzed around inside my head like angry flies. My mind suddenly shifted gears, catapulting me back down into the sawdust belly of an animal with a thousand eyes. Lights came on; the animal laughed at the stunted figure in Center Ring. I went into my act, hurling my body through a maze of trampolines, springboards, ropes and bars; the animal gasped and clapped its hands. When I finished, it cheered; but as always, the echo of that terrible laughter remained as a reminder that for me the price of being taken seriously is a good performance.

Statler spotted me. He stretched out his arms, grinned and shuffled forward with a rolling gait not unlike that of one of his trained bears. "Mongo!" he rasped, pumping my hand. "Mongo the Magnificent! How are you?"

Knowing Statler, I couldn't be sure whether he was asking about my health or my skills. The pleasure I was experiencing at seeing him again came as a mild shock. He smelled of circus, but I didn't know whether the odor was in my nose or in my imagination; I suspected I smelled the same to him. "I'm fine, Phil," I said, still groggy with memory. "And you look great, as if you'd just stolen an act from Ringling Brothers."

He scraped his fingers over a gray, two-day stubble of beard and shook his head thoughtfully. His teeth were his own, but uneven and tobacco-stained. His face was florid, marbled with broken veins. Even the colors of his pale, watery eyes didn't quite match. He wasn't an example of classical beauty; but he was honest, and he was fair. He was also crafty—maybe the best of the vanishing breed of modern-day circus men. But he plied his trade only with other professionals; Phil Statler didn't run games on rubes.

"Talent's gruel-thin these days," he said in a tone that was uncharacteristically soft, almost sad. "Ain't like it used to be; ain't much competition, even at the bottom, and the few good acts left are going stale. They don't compete against themselves the way you did. Hell, even when you can patch together a good show, the people won't come out. The spirit ain't the same, if you know what I mean."

The circus was a dying institution, I thought, a faint chuckle in the throat of a world gnawing on its own entrails. Kids no longer ran away to join the circus; now they shot dope, or returned to live on the land in garishly painted buses, or picked up a gun. Not all—certainly fewer than in the '60s—but still enough to make a difference. There were too many cold, hungry people in the darkness outside the tents, men and women with neither tickets nor talent. One day, perhaps, when the more obvious and persistent warts had been burned off the face of the country, there would again be a time and place for clowns and trapeze performers.

"How long are you in town, Phil?"

"Two weeks. We open at the Garden tomorrow." He looked at the palms of his gnarled hands, then gestured at the buildings around us. "You really teach here?"

"Sure. They tell me I'm an assistant professor."

"I heard you were some kind of doctor."

"No black bag. I have a Ph.D. in criminology."

"I also heard you hire out as a private detective."

"Yeah, but business isn't exactly booming. There are days when I'm not sure the world is ready for a dwarf private detective."

He laughed shortly. "So? Why do you do it?"

"My brother claims I overcompensate."

"Monkeyshit, my friend. You just happen to be a dwarf with a King Kong ego." His grin faded. "How come I had to learn all about you secondhand, Mongo? As far as I know, I always treated you square. I thought we were friends. A man wants to leave when his contract's up, that's his business; it's just that you seemed in a pretty big hurry."

"I'm sorry I haven't been in touch, Phil. I was running. I didn't say anything to you because . . ." My words trailed off, smothered by guilt. I owed Phil Statler, and I could find no way to tell him how I'd loathed every minute of my life with the circus. "There's no excuse, Phil," I finished lamely. "I'd earned my degree in the off season, and I had an offer to teach. The detective business came later."

Statler shrugged his massive shoulders. "Well, like I said, it ain't none of my business. I was afraid I'd said or done something you took personal."

"No, Phil. It was just bad manners on my part."

"How about coming back, pal?" The sudden offer took me by surprise, and Statler took my silence for indecision. "Knowing you, a few years haven't taken away that much. A

15

little work and you'd be back in top form, a headliner again. Uh, I might even be willing to discuss a percentage deal. I'm betting your name will still draw crowds."

"Forget it, Phil," I said quietly. "I don't perform in a ring for anyone anymore. I like being plain Bob Frederickson, and I like my work. It's great seeing you, but if you came here looking for a circus performer you've wasted your time."

"Well, you can't blame a man for trying," Statler said with a shrug. He took a cigar from the pocket of his sweater and lighted it. It took two matches, and I was grateful for the pause. "Actually," he continued, flicking a stray piece of tobacco off his lip with the tip of his tongue, "I need a private detective. I want to hire you."

"You're kidding."

He didn't smile. "No, I'm not kidding. If you don't want *this* job, just say so."

"I'm all ears."

"Come on, then. I have to get something out of my car."

We cut across campus to the visitors' parking lot, where Statler retrieved a large manila envelope from the glove compartment of his battered pickup. Then we went up to my office, where Statler took an eight-by-ten-inch publicity photo from the envelope and placed it on my desk. "I want you to find this man for me," he said.

The photo was a head-and-shoulders shot of a man with the kind of thick, muscular neck that takes years of hard, patient training to develop. His eyes were bright, small and mean: tiny black periods bracketing a huge paragraph of a nose. It was an intelligent but closed face, seemingly devoid of emotion. He had a full head of thick, curly black hair. Something about the man seemed vaguely familiar.

"There's a puckered scar on his right cheek," Phil said, tapping the print with his forefinger. "The photo's been retouched."

"Ornery-looking fellow. Who is he?"

"His name's Hassan Khordad." Statler produced a folded paper from the envelope and flattened it out in front of me. "That's what he looks like, and this is what he does."

The paper was a typical circus flyer—bad art, but good publicity. A reasonable likeness of Hassan Khordad was pictured straining beneath a wooden platform supporting four half-naked dancing girls. The large central illustration was ringed by a series of smaller ones which depicted Khordad performing a variety of juggling stunts with two huge, paddle-shaped blades. The act looked unusual, and very impressive.

"Headliner?" I asked.

He nodded. "We needed a star, and Khordad filled the bill. I spent a lot of money building him up. Then last month he took off on me."

Suddenly I knew why Khordad looked familiar. "Iranian?"

"Yeah," Statler said. "Persian, Iranian, I guess it's the same thing. How the hell did you know?"

"He just *looks* Iranian."

"*Looks* Iranian? Except for Khordad, I wouldn't know a Persian from a Pakistani."

"I have an Iranian friend here at the university, and my brother's into a heavy number with a veritable Persian princess. They do have a look about them. Where'd you lose yours?"

"Chicago, two weeks ago. March fifteenth, to be exact."

"He just took off?"

"Not exactly. We were scheduled to go on to Atlanta the next day. Khordad asked me for permission to skip the last show. He claimed he was having trouble with the Immigration people; something to do with his residency permit. Said he had to go to New York to straighten it out. What could I do? By that time he represented a heavy investment that would go right down the tubes if he got tossed out of the country. He was only supposed to be gone a couple of days,

17

so he just took a small bag. When he didn't show in Atlanta I figured he'd found more trouble than he'd bargained for, so I called the Immigration people. They claimed they'd never heard of him."

"Have you talked to the police?"

"Sure," Statler said. "But we're circus people; you know how much looking the police are going to do."

"Chances are he'd still wind up with his name on a list. That could be some help if he got busted or ended up in a hospital."

"Maybe, maybe not. An Iranian strongman isn't some rich man's missing daughter." He coughed and looked at his hands. "Besides, I don't want the police sticking their noses in too far."

"Why not?"

"Maybe he doesn't need the attention. If he is in some kind of trouble with the government, I don't want to be the one to blow the whistle on him."

"All right, Phil, so you're missing an act. Persians are very chauvinistic; maybe Khordad got homesick. Why throw good money after bad? Spend it on another muscle man."

Statler grunted. "You're not going to get rich off that kind of sales pitch."

"I like to think I look after the best interests of my clients. I'd love to take your money, but right now it seems to me you'd be better off using it to buy another act."

Statler shook his head. "There aren't any more acts like this one. Khordad wasn't just a muscle man; he had *class*. And that routine must have taken him ten years to develop. That's why I spent a few grand promoting him, building him into a headliner. If necessary, I'll spend a few grand more to find out what happened to him. If he's in trouble, I'll see what I can do to help him out of it."

"And if he's not in any trouble?"

"Then I'll damn well give him some. He broke a contract.

If you find out he's just shacking up with some broad, I'll run him out of the country personally."

"That's clear enough." It was pure Statler. Phil would break his back to help one of his people out of a jam; take advantage of him, and he'd break yours. "Where'd you pick him up?"

"Two years ago at the winter camp in Florida. He'd written me a letter—"

"He speaks and writes English?"

"Better than I do. He said he wanted to organize his own national circus back in Iran—I suppose something along the lines of the Moscow Circus. He claimed he had his government's backing, but he needed administrative experience. He wanted to learn the nuts and bolts of putting together a circus. He had one of the best acts I've ever seen, and I hired him on the spot. He was under contract to me for three years. He left a year early."

"Had he ever taken off before?"

"Not without permission. Last October he went back to Iran for two weeks. He was invited to some big blowout for that king they've got over there."

"The Shah?"

"Yeah, that's the guy."

I stared at the picture for a few moments, then shoved it back across the desk. "I'll be honest with you, Phil. I still think you should save your money and wait to see if the police turn up anything."

"What's the matter? You can't get away from here?"

"I can make arrangements, but that's not the point. This kind of thing can get expensive. You say he left Chicago two weeks ago to come here to New York. He could be anywhere now—even back in Iran."

"I don't think so. He wouldn't leave all his equipment behind."

"Even so, Phil, New York's a big place. Someone like your

man has no roots here. It could take months just to find someone who knew him, *if* anyone knew him."

"I know he had a friend here."

"In New York?"

"*Here*, at this school. That's why I waited until we got to New York, and that's why I want you." He grinned crookedly. "I can't wait to see Mongo the Magnificent do his new private-detective act."

"You inspire unbounded confidence. What makes you think Khordad knew somebody here at the university?"

"He had a visitor a few months back, in Cleveland. Fellow came to the stage door asking to see Khordad. He had a permanent pass—you know: the kind we give to all the performers for their friends. Johnny asked to see some identification, and this guy showed him a student I.D. card from this university. It stuck in Johnny's mind because Khordad kept pretty much to himself. As far as we knew, he didn't know anybody in this country."

I reached across the desk and pulled the photo back toward me. "Did you tell that to the police?"

"Sure. It didn't make much difference. They figured like you did: he got homesick."

"Does Johnny remember this friend's name?"

Statler shook his head. "It was foreign."

"What did he look like?"

"Late twenties, maybe. He was wearing dark glasses and a hat, so Johnny didn't get too good a look at him. Johnny says he thinks the guy's skin was olive, like an Indian's."

"Or a Persian's."

"Maybe. What about it, Mongo?"

I shrugged. "If you're determined to spend your money, I'd be a fool to send you someplace else. I'll give you my special ex-boss rates, but you're still not going to like them. A hundred a day when I'm on the job."

"Done," Statler said with a grin. "We'll be at the Garden

for a week, and I'll leave a number where you can reach me after we leave."

"How about a drink, Phil? There's a good bar just around the corner."

"Another time, Mongo. We've got a matinee at two. Hey, why don't you come around and catch the show? Johnny and the rest of the crowd would love to see you."

"Give me a rain check. I want to see if I can get a line on your strongman's friend."

The last time I'd been in the Statler Brothers Circus was as a performer—a gifted freak who'd become a headliner. I wasn't ready to go back yet, even to visit. Perhaps Phil understood. We shook hands and he walked out of the office, closing the door quietly behind him. It occurred to me that it was April Fool's Day; I hoped it wasn't significant.

2

AFTER CHECKING IN the university directory, I cut across campus toward the building housing the offices of an outfit calling itself the Confederation of Iranian Students. I took my time. Statler had struck a few raw nerves and I was preoccupied with ghosts. Phil was a shrewd man, and there had been an unspoken thought behind his words throughout our conversation: regardless of my academic qualifications, I didn't belong at a university; I belonged in a circus. I didn't believe it, but it bothered me that Phil might.

The circus had been good to me, had fed me and even brought me a measure of fame. But there'd been complications; Nature had compounded the irony of my birth by endowing me with an I.Q. that on a good day, so I was told, hovered a notch or two above the norm. I'd also been told I was ambitious. Being a smart, ambitious dwarf can get tedious, and my drives and frustrations eventually landed me on a series of psychiatrists' couches. That phase of my life lasted as long as it took me to discover that the average psychiatrist was more neurotic than I was.

Books came next. Eventually I earned my doctorate in criminology—no doubt as a means of scratching some perverse psychic itch. Meanwhile, the university and I had made the mutual discovery that I was a good teacher, and that had led to an offer of a teaching position. My satisfaction lasted about a month; teaching had provided me an escape from the circus, but it wasn't enough. I hadn't been able to stand the security. I'd longed for the blood and sweat of the marketplace. Six months after I'd accepted a teaching position, I had my private investigator's license and a downtown office which, exactly as in the movies, consisted of dirty windows, a desk, two chairs and an answering service. Occasionally I even had a client.

My brother, Garth—like me a refugee from the flat, golden landscapes, warm people and deadly boredom of the Nebraska corn belt—tended to find all this postcircus activity faintly amusing. He could afford to, since he wasn't suffering the disastrous effects of a recessive gene three generations old. A strapping six feet two inches tall, Garth was a lieutenant in the Plainclothes Division of the New York City Police Department.

The office of the Confederation of Iranian Students was located in the basement of a sciences building on the western edge of the campus. It was presided over by a very attractive girl sitting behind a scarred desk piled high with what looked like cheaply printed political tracts. Her eyes were large, moist, black as her raven hair and with the same mysterious slivers of light flashing through them. I cleared my throat. The girl looked up and smiled brightly, exposing a line of white teeth that were a perfect complement to her hair and eyes, and to the earth-brown flesh of her face.

"Hello, Dr. Frederickson."

It's hard to remain anonymous when you're the only dwarf professor on campus, but I was still flattered. "*Salaam,*" I said, watching for her reaction. "Uh, *hale shoma chetore?*"

"Khube! Merci!" the girl said, beaming. *"Shoma?"*

"I'm fine," I replied, "but that's the extent of my Persian vocabulary, except for a few pungent colloquialisms which I'll spare you."

"Where did you learn Farsi?"

"Oh, I've picked up a few words from Dr. Khayyam."

Her eyes clouded. "Dr. Khayyam?"

"He's a friend of mine. We play chess once or twice a month."

"Oh."

Her smile fluttered and was gone. Since I didn't consider our earlier brief queries about the state of each other's health very controversial, I assumed it was the mention of Khayyam's name that had dampened what looked like a promising friendship. I wondered why. Darius Khayyam was the chairman of the Department of Middle Eastern Studies. As far as I knew, he rarely mentioned Iran or Iranians outside his class. A thickness in his speech that could have been pain whenever the subject came up had led me to suspect that his reluctance could be the result of some intense personal suffering, and I'd never pressed. But it seemed that Darius and the girl weren't on the best of terms.

"You and Dr. Khayyam don't get along?"

"It's not that," she said, averting her gaze. "We . . . tend to avoid unnecessary contact with Dr. Khayyam."

"Hmm. Sounds political."

"I'd rather not discuss it," she said quietly.

"What's your name?" I asked, anxious to get the conversation back to higher ground.

"Anna. Anna Najafi."

"Anna's a beautiful name, but it doesn't sound very Iranian."

The girl flushed. "It is short for Andalib."

"Well, Anna, I hope you'll teach me more Farsi." That

helped some; she was smiling again, and I pressed my advantage. "How did you know *my* name?"

Anna seemed surprised. "Why, everyone knows *you*, Dr. Frederickson. You should see the scramble at the beginning of every semester to get a seat in one of your sections."

"I'm sorry I haven't seen you in one of those sections."

She giggled. "I'm a graduate student in microbiology, and I don't have any electives. If I did, you can be sure I'd be there."

"Anna," I said, sensing that we seemed to be back on speaking terms, "I'm hoping that you can help me; I'm looking for someone. Does the name Hassan Khordad mean anything to you?"

Anna thought for a moment, then shook her head. "No. It's an Iranian name and I'd recognize it if he were a student here."

"He's not a student, but he may know one." I showed her the publicity photo. "This is what he looks like."

She studied the photo, then handed it back. "I'm sorry, Dr. Frederickson. I don't know him. I'd remember a face like that."

"You're sure? You've never seen him on campus?"

"No."

"The photo's been retouched," I persisted. "He has a scar on his right cheek."

The girl shrugged. "So do thousands of other Iranians. It is a *salaak*, a scar left by a virus infection peculiar to Iran."

So much for the scar. "Do you know any students who are interested in circuses or weight lifting?"

"I don't understand."

"The man I'm looking for worked in a circus. Before that he'd done a lot of weight lifting. He may have known someone at the university, and I thought the key to their relationship might be a common interest."

"Ali Azad is the vice-president of our organization," Anna said, an odd catch in her voice. "I'll call him. He may be able to help you." Anna picked up the phone on her desk and dialed a number. She spoke in rapid Farsi, occasionally glancing up at me. I heard my name mentioned twice, along with Darius Khayyam and another name that I didn't quite catch but which had a familiar ring to it. She finished and turned her attention back to me. "I caught him just as he was leaving," Anna said, hanging up. The lights in her eyes had gone out; her voice was crisp and polite, but distant.

"Thank you."

"You're welcome," she replied coldly. She gestured toward some papers on her desk. "Please excuse me, Dr. Frederickson. I have work to do before I go to class. Ali will be here in a few minutes."

She abruptly began shuffling papers in a way that precluded any further conversation. Her mercurial shifts in mood fascinated me; once again I'd apparently struck the wrong key on a strange instrument I was playing blindfolded. I settled myself into a chair and looked around.

Except for the stacks of political pamphlets and a rundown mimeograph machine in one corner, the office was clean and uncluttered. There was a closed door to the left of Anna's desk. The walls of the office were covered with posters, most of them radical leftist in nature; Che Guevara stared down at me from a variety of revolutionary poses. There was a large, trick blowup of a man sitting on a toilet seat and reading a comic book; even without the crown on his head I recognized the Shah of Iran. There seemed little doubt what place the Confederation of Iranian Students occupied in the political spectrum.

The entire upper half of one wall was covered by a huge, multipaneled photograph of the most magnificent ruins I'd ever seen. I would have liked to ask what and where they were, but the atmosphere in the room was still tense and I decided to leave well enough alone. There was a ghostly aura about the ruins, a visual magnetism that imparted a faint sensation of vertigo, a feeling of Time and Space transcended. In the foreground, two huge pillars thrust up into the sky; atop one, a sheared section of stone that must have weighed several tons was balanced precariously, defying the centuries' insistence that it fall.

When I turned back to Anna, I caught her watching me out of the corner of her eye. I rose and walked to her desk. "Anna, something I said upset you. Please tell me what it was."

She glanced up, but whatever she was going to say was cut off by the sound of a door opening and closing behind me.

"*I* will talk to you, Dr. Frederickson."

Turning toward the sound of the voice, I found myself looking into a pair of gleaming brown eyes with a hot brilliance only slightly damped by the large horn-rimmed glasses the man wore. He was short, only a foot or so taller than I was, but tension crackled about him like static electricity; he seemed like a taut guy wire ready to snap under one more turn of some emotional winch. I put his age at around twenty-five: probably a graduate student working for his Ph.D. His skin was darker than Anna's; a goatee and pencil-thin moustache lent him a sinister, Mephisphelean air that he obviously cultivated.

"I am Ali Azad," he said, stepping forward and grasping my hand firmly. He sounded like a diplomat greeting an enemy negotiator. "Your reputation precedes you. I'm glad we have this chance to meet."

"You don't sound too sure."

He didn't smile. His eyes bored into mine, but I held his gaze. "How welcome you are depends on your real reason for being here."

"Didn't Anna tell you? I'm looking for a man, an Iranian."

"Why?"

"He's not where he's supposed to be."

"That doesn't answer my question," he said sharply. "Why should a missing Iranian interest you?"

"I was hired to find him."

"Whom are you working for?"

"A client."

"What is his name?"

"That doesn't concern you," I said evenly. The questioning had become a bit too one-sided, and Azad's hostility had ruffled my usually benevolent demeanor.

"But you would have *me* bandy about the names of student members!" he snapped. His eyes grew rounder, bright with unbridled passion. "How much does the C.I.A. pay you?"

He'd snuck up on me with that one. My consternation must have shown on my face, because Azad dropped his eyes and began to seem less sure of himself.

"Look," I said, "I obviously make you nervous, but I'm damned if I know why. I've been accused of a lot of things, but never of passing a physical for the C.I.A. I came here looking for information that might help me find a man who's disappeared. That's all. I certainly can't force you to co-operate, so I think we're both wasting our time." It had the right ring for an exit line, and I headed for the door. Azad's voice stopped me.

"Please wait, Dr. Frederickson," he said. I turned with my hand still on the knob. The Iranian made a gesture that could have been broadly interpreted as an apology. He nodded toward the closed door. "We can talk in the other room without being interrupted."

The door by Anna's desk led into a smaller inner office, and I followed Ali Azad into it. There was a screen door at the opposite end looking out on a small patio piled high with garbage cans. He motioned for me to sit down on a lumpy couch. I remained standing.

With all the psychological undercurrents swirling around the girl, Azad and me, I was having trouble keeping my mind on why I'd come in the first place. I showed him the photograph. "His name's Hassan Khordad," I said. "I thought you or someone else might have seen him on campus."

He seemed to be only half-looking at the picture, and I had the impression his thoughts were racing ahead of him. "I don't know him," Azad said quietly. Sweat had dewed his moustache; he swallowed and licked his lips. "You mentioned something to Anna about this man being a weight lifter."

I unfolded the circus poster and handed it to him. Thin, white lines suddenly appeared in the dark flesh around the corners of his mouth. "There's reason to believe he had a friend here at the university. A student."

"I don't believe that!" he said tersely, his fingers curling like talons around the edges of the poster. "I know every Iranian at this school. Not one of the students would be a friend to this man."

"How can you be so sure?"

"Because I know what this man is." His voice had fallen to a soft, hate-filled hiss. "He is a *chagu-kesh*."

"What's a *chagu-kesh*?"

Azad eyed me intently. "I'm still not convinced you don't already know."

"In which case it wouldn't hurt for *you* to tell me, would it? But I don't know."

He stepped to the door looking out on the patio. A light breeze wafted in, bringing the smell of flowers struggling somewhere out in the early spring. "Literally translated, it means 'someone who draws a knife.' It is a Persian term for a thief or murderer. If you want to know the place of men like

29

this in recent Iranian history, you should ask your friend Dr. Khayyam. He lived a part of it." He sucked in his breath, slowly let it out. "His sister *died* a part of it."

The information intrigued me; Darius had never mentioned a sister. But I noted the animosity in the student leader's voice and decided I wanted no part of whatever feud existed between my friend and the student group.

"Dr. Khayyam is just a professor now. I'm here, so why don't you tell me?"

There was a long silence during which Azad continued to stare out the door. I waited. "The man you're looking for is—or was—obviously a member of the *Zur-khaneh*," he said at last. These are men totally dedicated to physical fitness. The weights, weapons and wooden paddles they use in the rituals they perform are part of a kind of national exercise that dates back centuries. In a very real sense, these athletes are part of Iran's cultural heritage; they perform for state occasions and visiting dignitaries. They spend much of their time in the *Zur-khaneh*, a special gymnasium in Tehran." He paused, cleared his throat self-consciously. "Most of them are deeply religious."

"Except when they go around killing people?"

His eyes were flashing when he wheeled to face me. "I am trying to be honest with you! Are you mocking me?"

"No, Azad," I said, suppressing a sigh. "I'm listening."

"There is a small group of men selected from the *Zur-khaneh* who serve as the Shah's personal bodyguard. They're a personal army, and they're very well taken care of. Those are the men I mentioned; it was those murderers who helped bring the Shah back to power after the people had forced him to leave the country. You must have heard about that."

"A little." I knew more than a little, but I wanted Azad's version of events, unfettered by what he thought I knew. "When did all this take place?"

"I'm surprised Dr. Khayyam hasn't mentioned it."

"He hasn't."

"In 1921 the present Shah's father, Reza Shah, seized power from the Qajar dynasty in a *coup d'état*." He paused, added wryly, "Not that it made much difference. Iran in the twentieth century has always been controlled by foreign powers because of its oil and its strategic geographical location—first by the British, then by the Americans. In 1941 the Allies removed Reza Shah and installed the son in his place."

"Why?"

"The war. There was our oil, and Iran represented a land bridge to Russia for essential supplies. The Allies were worried about Iran's neutrality, and they thought they could ensure Iran's security by installing Reza Shah's twenty-year-old son on the throne as their puppet. After the war the Western powers found it convenient to leave the son in power because the cold war had begun and Iran represented a bulwark in the Middle East *against* the Russians. In the meantime the British continued to bleed us of oil, and there wasn't anybody in a position to do anything about it until 1950, when Mohammed Mossadegh was elected Premier."

"And who supported Mossadegh?"

"The *people!*" Azad said fiercely, clenching and unclenching his fists; he was in a world of his own, a warrior in a battle that had taken place when he was no more than an infant. "The people *loved* Mossadegh, and eventually he became even more popular than the Shah. In May of 1951, Mossadegh nationalized the oil industry. That enraged the British and the Americans, but it made him a giant in the eyes of most Iranians. By 1953 he had assumed complete control of the country by acclamation. The Shah was asked to abdicate or become a constitutional monarch; he panicked and flew to Rome."

"Obviously, he found his way back again."

Azad laughed bitterly. "He most certainly did—thanks to

the C.I.A. Mossadegh was overthrown in 1953. That was accomplished by C.I.A. operatives who paid out millions of dollars in bribes to men like the one you search for; they acted as conduits for the money, bribing thousands of ignorant peasants and laborers to agitate against Mossadegh. Those who didn't go along were beaten or killed. Within a few days, the Shah was back in power.

"Hundreds of army officers and government officers were executed. Dr. Khayyam's sister was an assistant minister. She was raped by a dozen soldiers, imprisoned and then burned alive in her cell. The official report called it suicide, but no one was expected to believe it. Her death was meant to serve as a lesson to others."

I said nothing. I was thinking of Darius, and his terrible grief weaving a tapestry of pain that had finally folded in upon itself, producing a bitter silence on matters concerning his native country.

"Now it is Mohammed Reza Pahlavi who is in complete control of Iran," Azad continued. "The United States supports him because he guarantees order, but nevertheless any dissent in Iran is paid for in blood."

"Okay," I said. "I've read accounts of torture in Iranian prisons."

"*Read accounts?*" Ali hissed contemptuously. "You cannot appreciate the horror of Iranian torture chambers by reading accounts. You know nothing of these things."

He was wrong. I had no intention of discussing it, but I had more than a passing acquaintance with torture. A year and a half before, I'd been searching for a man by the name of Victor Rafferty who just happened to be, among other things, a total telepath—and thus a kind of Ultimate Weapon in the eyes of the various intelligence communities. I'd been competing with the Russians, Americans, French and British, and I'd been unlucky enough to fall into the hands of a Russian man-monster by the name of Kaznakov;

it was Kaznakov who'd taught me a few things about the calculus of mental and physical agony. If it hadn't been for the near-miraculous healing powers of Victor Rafferty, I'd have ended as a catatonic staring out the barred windows of some mental institution.

Kaznakov had gotten his when I'd barbecued him with an incendiary grenade during the course of a raid on the Russian Consulate in New York. But the psychic scar tissue from Kaznakov's lesson still remained to stretch, prickle and throb whenever the subject of torture came up.

"Let's get back to this Hassan Khordad," I said, pushing away the memory. "Why can't Khordad be nothing more than what he appears to be? Why can't he be one of the good guys?"

Azad's laughter was thin and choked. "This man is an assassin, a butcher for the Shah. Believe me. Men like him sold the freedom of our nation for a few dirty American dollars. That is why no student at this university would waste spit on such a man."

I was getting only Azad's side of the story. I thought of some of the insane fringe groups in my own country and wondered how much of Azad's account could have been tainted by his own brand of political paranoia. Being in no position to judge, I didn't. "Even assuming that this Khordad is a killer, isn't it conceivable that one of your members could *still* be a friend of his?"

"No. Not unless—"

"Not unless one of your members might not be as anti-Shah as you'd like to believe?"

"I meant nothing," he snapped. Visibly upset, he suddenly began to pace. His accent had become noticeably more pronounced.

"You still haven't told me why you're so positive Khordad is what you say he is."

He wheeled and held up the poster. His hands were shaking, making the paper rattle. "Why shouldn't he be any more than what he appears to be? Appears to whom? To *you*, Dr. Frederickson? I've told you that you know nothing of these things!"

"I won't argue with that."

"Whatever this man's stated reason for being in this country, it is probably a lie. A member of the *Zur-khaneh* has no reason to leave Iran; life is very good for them there."

"He wants to have his own circus."

"A fairy tale," Azad snorted.

"All right, why do *you* think he came here? Let's see if you can be a little more specific."

"I told you: he's here as an errand boy for the Shah."

"But what—"

"I can't talk to you anymore," he said, forcing the words through clenched teeth. There were tears in his eyes, tears of rage—or something else that I could not yet comprehend.

"There's more to this business, isn't there?" I asked quietly. "Why can't you tell me what it is?"

"Go look for your man in some sewer!"

My interview with Ali Azad was obviously over, and I walked into the outer office. Anna glanced up at me and smiled nervously. On the opposite wall, pools of reflected fluorescent light danced across the photograph of the ruins. In one corner of the picture the torso of a two-headed bull rested in the dust on its crumbled haunches. Behind it stood the remnants of an archway with men and animals carved into its stone facade. There were other such columns and monuments marching off into the distance where they came to an abrupt halt at the base of a series of steep foothills. Even on the backdrop of mountains men had left their mark, but the mountains were too far away for me to determine exactly what form the marks had taken. As I stared at this surreal jumble, it suddenly struck me that I was dealing with people from a culture that was very old, very complex, and

—perhaps—finally beyond the ken of an American who'd actually considered it a big deal when his own country had celebrated its two-hundredth birthday.

"There's one more thing I'd like to ask you," I said, turning back to the young man.

"I've said too much already. I'll speak no more of this matter."

"What was happening in Iran last October?"

Azad's smile was more a grimace; his eyes remained smooth crystals of brown ice. "You might call it a celebration of a celebration."

"You're being obtuse."

"You remember the twenty-five-hundredth-year celebration?"

"I do."

"Oh, that was a sight," he said mockingly. "The world's greatest collection of freeloaders all gathered together in one spot, supposedly to honor Iran but eating *French* food flown in every day specially for the occasion. Anyway, the biggest thing in Iran last October was an art festival commemorating that celebration. I assume that's what you're referring to."

"I'm not sure what I was referring to, but I think you've answered my question."

"God, how I hate the arrogance of that man!" Azad spat out. "In a nation where the infant mortality rate is more than fifty percent, where eighty percent of the population is illiterate and more than half do not have enough to eat, our *Shahanshah*, our *glorious* King of Kings and Light of the Aryans, spent more than fifty million dollars to celebrate twenty-five hundred years of monarchy."

3

ALI AZAD HAD GIVEN ME a lot of heat on Iranian politics, but nothing but smoke on Phil Statler's missing strongman. At the moment I wasn't prepared to take too much of what the Iranian had said at face value; the man was simply too emotional. It was time to talk to Darius.

The professor wasn't in his office, and when I called his home there was no answer. I still had two hours before I was scheduled to teach a seminar; not wanting to waste them, I climbed into my Volkswagen and drove uptown to my brother's precinct. I was told he was having lunch in the small restaurant across the street.

I was happy for the excuse to see Garth. The pressure cooker that was New York City was making strangers of us, and I regretted it. Garth, along with my parents, had been the calm eye in the storm of family tragedy that had been my birth. While my other relatives were moaning and debating which limb of the family tree I'd dropped from, my parents had been buying me books and Garth had been reading them to me; Garth had carried me on his shoulders, literally and figuratively, across the bleak, lunar landscape of my childhood, leaving behind a trail of broken noses attesting to his touchiness on the subject of jokes about his dwarf brother. It was this simple kindness toward another human being who was at the same time a source of considerable embarrassment that would always mark Garth, in my eyes, as a truly great man. I loved him, and wished that life could be as kind to him as he'd been to me.

He'd married young, only to see his wife and twin baby daughters killed in a highway smashup a year and a half later; the loss had seemed to jerk his life permanently off track. Although on the surface he seemed to carry his grief well, I always knew better. His scars had never healed, and he'd traded the isolation of being a sheriff in the Great Plains country for the even greater isolation of being a police detective in the jungle of glass and steel that was New York City. A compleat professional, he was nonetheless—to those who knew him—a lonely, shy man prone to spells of deep depression and chronic insomnia.

But he'd been deliriously happy—and, I assumed, sleeping like an exhausted lover—for the past few weeks, and the reason for this rejuvenated mental health was sitting next to Garth's gaunt, rawboned frame at a rear table in the restaurant. Neptune Tabrizi was five feet five of Middle East exotica; physical perfection except, perhaps, for a little plumpness in the bust—which was just fine for a confirmed breast man like my brother. Neptune was thirty-nine, and her jet black hair was naturally streaked with individual gray hairs, providing her with an ebony-and-silver crown that no hairdresser in the world could have matched. She had almond-colored eyes, olive skin and a full mouth with perfect teeth; the constant laughter in her face and voice was the only makeup she'd ever need. She worked for the Celanese Corporation, and she'd met Garth when he'd investigated the burglary of her Riverside Plaza apartment in early February.

They'd been inseparable ever since. As far as I was concerned, Neptune was the best thing that had ever happened to Garth—and that included his first wife, whom I'd never much liked anyway.

"Company!" I announced, executing a little two-step in front of their table.

"Company," Garth groaned, while Neptune giggled and clapped her hands.

"Hello, beautiful," I said, kissing Neptune on the cheek.

She put her hand behind my neck and kissed me on the mouth. "Hello, you precious little thing."

I sighed and put my hand over my heart. "You're the only person in the world who could call me a precious little thing and not make me want to hit them."

Garth picked up a table knife and grinned wickedly. "Neptune's the only person in the world who'd think you were precious—little thing."

"*Arrgh!* Gasp! Choke!" I snatched up Neptune's knife and fenced with my brother until we'd managed to disturb the entire restaurant, at which point I made an apologetic bow to the angry manager and sat down next to Neptune.

"You're both *crazy!*" Neptune whispered with delight.

"Has my brother found your jewelry yet?"

She shook her head. "And here I thought I could assure myself of special treatment by falling in love with the investigating detective."

That made Garth uncomfortable, although I didn't think Neptune noticed. "Who's minding the ivory tower, brother?" he asked me.

"That task has fallen to my subordinates for the day," I said archly. "I am exploring the world of the great unwashed, the selfless guardians of our society."

"And what role are we playing today?"

"I have shed my cloak of anonymous, mild-mannered professor to reveal my true identity."

Garth almost smiled. "That would be Master Investigator?"

"You've got it."

The waiter brought salad and looked inquiringly at me. I shook my head.

"Bad week for investigators," Garth said seriously. "Day before yesterday we fished a colleague of yours out of the East River."

"Who?"

"John Simpson. You know him?"

"No."

Garth shrugged and wiped his mouth with his napkin. "What are you working on?"

"I thought you'd never ask. I'm looking for a missing Iranian." I showed him Khordad's photograph. "His name's Hassan Khordad. I wanted to check the Missing Persons and morgue sheets."

"You have his stats?"

"They're on the back of the photo."

Garth flipped the photograph over and studied the information sheet taped to the back. Neptune had pushed her salad to one side and was watching him with intense interest. "Performer?" Garth asked.

"Circus; muscle act."

Garth copied the name and stats in his pocket pad and handed me back the photo. "I'll check it out. Get back to me this afternoon."

"God, I've never seen you so cooperative. It must be love. By the way: if it makes any difference, he was supposed to be on his way to New York when he dropped out of sight."

"Mongo should try The Santur," Neptune said to Garth.

"What's that?" I asked.

Neptune touched my hand. "It's a nightclub just down the street. If your man's Iranian and he's been anywhere near the city, chances are he may have shown up there at least once. Someone may know him or remember seeing him there." She turned to Garth. "Garth, let's go with him."

"Uh, I had other plans for this evening, sweetheart."

She squeezed his arm hard. "But I'd really *like* to go," she said seriously. "It's all very exciting."

Garth shot me an icy warning look; Garth was horny.

"Sorry, beautiful," I said, rising, "but I never mix business with pleasure. With you along, I wouldn't be able to concentrate on my incredibly exciting, perilous work. Thanks, folks. See you."

After shaving and showering at my apartment, I went downstairs and had copies made of Khordad's photo. Then I drove back over to the university to teach my seminar. In the evening I phoned Garth, who told me that Khordad's name was on an M.P. list from Chicago, but that was all. His body wasn't in the morgue, so it looked as though I'd have to do things the hard way, as usual.

I called a cab, which took me across town. I found The Santur tucked away between a dry-cleaning store and an antique shop. The club was a puddle of laughter in the middle of an otherwise somber neighborhood that barricaded itself behind thick ribbons of steel when darkness came. Neon and music dribbled out into the darkened street; it was still early in the evening, but a steady stream of people flowed back and forth through the painted doors.

Inside, I found myself sucked into the middle of a milling crowd where all attempts at conversation vied with a wailing din of Eastern music. I steered toward the sound of clinking glasses to my left, wedged myself into a corner of the bar and managed to signal the bartender.

From the vantage point of my bar stool, I sipped my Scotch on the rocks and studied the layout of the club. There was a slightly elevated platform in the bar area near the entrance; to the rear was a large dining area and dance floor. The music came from a stage to the right of the dance floor, where a group of dark-skinned Middle Eastern musicians held forth. The lead instrument was some kind of reed affair which sounded like a cross between a saxophone and an oboe, its intricate rhythms flitting, sweeping and dancing atop a steady beat laid down by a set of what looked like bongo drums, but were larger.

After a few minutes the closeness of the room, the Scotch and the strange, haunting quality of the atonal music began to have an effect; I whooped along with the others at a particularly exciting passage of music. People stared, but strangers usually stared; I simply nodded my head and stared back. It was a technique that invariably worked. The staring number finished, I continued my inspection of the club.

Like the bar, the dining and dancing area was jammed with people. Most of the faces looked foreign and were probably Iranian; they had the same dusky features and dark hair as the man whose picture I carried in my pocket. There were a few Americans—mostly tourist types, with one notable exception; this particular American was dressed in an expensive suit, and his gold watchband glittered somewhere in the vicinity of a thousand dollars. Barely holding his own against a waistline that was running to fat, he had a florid face that was bracketed by thick, reddish sideburns which only served to draw attention to the fact that the rest of his head was bald. I put his age at around fifty.

What set him apart were his dinner companions and his bearing; unlike the other Americans, he seemed completely at home in The Santur as he laughed and joked with the Iranian men and women on either side of him. Occasionally he would rise and dance with a woman. She wore a quarter-inch-wide gold wedding band; from the way they danced, I hoped she was the American's wife.

A man sitting alone at an adjacent table rose and staggered drunkenly toward the exit. I walked quickly across the room and sat down in his seat. The American's table was directly behind me.

The dancers were performing a type of circle dance, frequently stopping to clap their hands or stamp their feet as if to punctuate their difficult in-and-out, back-and-forth maneuvers. A few non-Iranians joined in, but they were clumsy and always at least a half beat behind the others. The man with the sideburns was the exception again; he moved gracefully with the music, anticipating every move, swaying with the rhythms. Finally the music soared to a crescendo, then stopped; the exhausted dancers began making their way back to their seats. The American and his Iranian wife, their faces flushed with heat and pleasure, passed close to my chair.

I smiled and spoke to the man. "That looks like a lot of fun, and you look right at home. I envy you."

The woman reacted first, lightly touching my arm and smiling. Her face, like Anna's, seemed to carry a vast reservoir of emotions close to the surface; her eyes were limpid and hot, too large for the rest of her face, which was thin and ethereal. She filled her dress well, but her magnetism was completely internal. The man projected the opposite image; his eyes were cold, polished green agates pushed into the puffy flesh of his face. Off the dance floor, up close, he seemed stiff and defensive, like a man who'd tried to buy the grace that sometimes comes with culture and been shortchanged. As he studied me his eyes seemed to constantly change focus, as though he were looking at me through a series of emotional lenses. Finally he smiled thinly and asked me something in Farsi.

"Sorry," I said, shaking my head, "I only know a few words. Actually, my interest in Iran is fairly recent—but growing fast."

"Well, you've come to the right place if you're interested

in Iran," the man said over the easy ripple of the woman's laughter.

"Here," the woman said, indicating an empty chair at their table. "Come and join us."

"Bob Frederickson," I said, extending my hand as I moved to the table. The man's grip was weak, bony and uneven for his size, as if his hand had been broken and never properly reset.

"Orrin Bannon," the man said. "This is my wife, Soussan."

The woman and I exchanged pleasantries; then I settled back in my seat and tried to think of a way to gracefully steer the conversation around to the picture and poster folded in my pocket. The band had left the stage for the bar, and the platform was now bare except for a single straight-backed chair and a low, broad bench. The lights blinked on and off.

Soussan Bannon leaned across her husband. "The man you're about to hear is the greatest santur player in the world," she whispered to me. "His name is Omar."

"Then a santur is something besides the name of this place?"

"Yes. It is an instrument. You will see."

Omar stepped from behind a green velvet curtain to my left and walked across the floor to the stage. A thin, short man with sharp, angular features and graying hair, he would have been lost in a crowd of three—except for the instrument he carried under his arm; its mere presence seemed to stiffen his spine, and he carried it as a man might carry his soul. The instrument consisted of a hollow wooden sounding board about a yard long and a foot wide. The surface of the board was covered with taut gut strings anchored on either side of the board by steel tuning pegs.

Omar cocked his head to one side and smiled shyly at the audience, then sat down and positioned his santur on the bench in front of him. He removed a metal device from his pocket and began an intricate tuning procedure with a fragile wooden mallet shaped like a toothbrush which he held in his other hand. Occasionally he would merely brush the strings with the side of the tiny mallet and the air would fill with a lush, enameled sound, like the whirring wings of a flock of metal birds.

There was no pause between tuning and actual performance; one merged into the other, until finally both hands held the delicate mallets which moved in a perpetual blur, like hummingbirds' wings, over the santur. Separate notes and chords were woven together into a curtain of sound that was exquisitely finespun, yet overwhelmingly powerful with a sinewy, achingly beautiful force that spoke to me of sadness, of mountains and heat and ruined, ghostly cities; I heard the terrible, deadly beauty that must be the soul of the desert.

The music, even the more spirited passages, seemed built on scales of sadness; the santur was a weeping instrument that worshiped the trinity of life, death and land, dripping tears over this triumvirate of existence that for the Iranian, I realized, must seem one. There was an air of immediacy to the music—thousands of split-second decisions enforced by a pair of flying hands building tiers of chords through which individual notes scampered and dipped like fragments of half-remembered dreams.

Then it was over, the last delicate chords drifting away like wisps of clouds. The lights came up. Somewhere behind me a woman was softly crying. Omar acknowledged the applause with a slight bow, then stood with his santur and walked back through the velvet curtain.

Bannon lighted a cigarette. "Did you like it?" he asked gruffly.

I tried to think of something original to say, and couldn't. "It was beautiful," I said simply. "I've never heard anything quite like it. Why isn't Omar in Iran? I wouldn't think there'd be much demand for santur players in the United States."

"There isn't, but there is some money in it for him here. More than in Iran."

"I thought it might be his politics," I said carefully.

Bannon took a long time to answer. "You didn't mention that you were interested in Iranian politics," he said quietly.

"Actually, I only know what I read in the newspapers or see on television."

"Oh? What do you read and see?" Bannon was staring into his drink.

"Well, I know that Pahlavi—" I stopped in mid-sentence. Soussan Bannon had stiffened; a couple at an adjacent table had paused in their conversation and were staring angrily at me. I was definitely in Shah Country. "Uh, the Shah," I continued, lowering my voice, "is a tough man to get a line on. On television—and you see a lot of him on television—he comes across as urbane, intelligent and tremendously proud of his country. He obviously loves Iran, and he spends an enormous amount of money here promoting it. But the day after some great puff piece in *Newsweek* his jailers will get caught torturing political prisoners, and all that expensive public relations work goes down the drain. Anyway, I know Iran is a police state, and I thought that might have something to do with a musician of Omar's caliber being here."

Bannon was half-turned in his seat and it was hard to tell what, if anything, was going on in his face. Soussan Bannon, perhaps sensing the tension in her husband's voice, was chatting determinedly with the woman next to her.

"Don't believe everything bad you hear about the Shah," Bannon said evenly. "Most of it's garbage."

As I was trying to think of a tactful way to frame my next question the lights dimmed again. A spotlight stabbed through the darkness, skittered across the floor and came to rest on the green curtain.

"Here's Leyla," Bannon continued tightly. "I think you'll find her more interesting than Iranian politics."

Once again the room was filled with the wailing music of the band, this time underlined by an even heavier drumbeat. The woman, clothed only in a brief halter and flowing silk trousers, leaped through a fold in the curtains, went rigid for a moment in the smoky cone of light, then bumped her hips to one side and raised her arms; suddenly the air was filled with the staccato clash of the tiny cymbals she wore on her fingers. She closed her eyes and stiffened, the spotlight caressing her body, the music of her cymbals challenging the drums and reeds.

Then Leyla began to dance, slowly at first, her body undulating in slow, peristaltic waves like some great, lovely serpent. Gradually the pace quickened and her breasts bounced in time to the music. Her flesh was moist; large droplets of perspiration oozed from her pores and ran in glistening rivulets down her body. The overall effect was electrifying, an erotic marriage of life and the earth.

I kept my eyes on the girl and leaned toward Bannon. "Iranian?"

Bannon shook his head. He smelled of expensive cologne and the musky odor of desire. "Egyptian," he said. "Iranian men are great connoisseurs of the belly dance, but they don't like their women doing it. Performers in Iran are looked down on."

He signaled to the waiter, who moved over and took our orders.

"Tell me," I said, "how does an American learn so much about Iran?"

Bannon touched his wife's shoulder solicitously. "My teacher."

"Mrs. Bannon is a lovely woman," I said, flashing my best Sunday smile. "How did the two of you meet?"

"Through my business," Bannon said. "I spend a great deal of time in Iran. I met Soussan there."

Hearing her name, the woman turned and patted her husband affectionately. Bannon smiled and kissed her gently on the cheek. Whatever his other faults, he had good taste in women.

"Tell me, Mr. Frederickson," Mrs. Bannon said, "what work do you do?"

"I teach criminology at N.Y.U." I decided not to mention the private-investigator business until I had to. I had no idea if Bannon could help me, but he seemed to be a regular at The Santur and he spoke my language; private detectives, like questions, tend to make people nervous, and I wanted to make certain I approached the subject properly.

Bannon grunted noncommittally; if he was surprised, he had the grace to hide it.

"You've piqued my curiosity," I said casually. "Aside from the torture, what are some of the other bad things I'm likely to hear about the Shah and his people?"

"Childish mouthings from people who should know better; people who talk about freedom when they mean anarchy."

"There must be a middle ground for discussion somewhere. Wouldn't you agree that Iran's a police state?"

"Sure," Bannon said, lighting a cigar, "but that's as it should be. You can't compare Iran to a country like the United States. There is *no* place like the United States. This country functions better as a democracy because it *developed* as a democracy. Iran, on the other hand, is better off as a monarchy—or police state, if you will."

"You're speaking as someone who enjoys all the freedoms of this country," I said, smiling so hard it hurt.

"I'm speaking as someone who knows Iran," he replied evenly.

Leyla danced on, her eyelids half-closed and fluttering, completely lost in the music. She came off the dance floor and began to writhe her way between the tables. Her body glistened. She seemed to take no notice of the hands that reached out and stuffed dollar bills into the moist cleft between her breasts.

Nor was it only the men who enjoyed Leyla's dancing. I'd stolen a glance at Soussan Bannon; the slim woman was sitting on the edge of her chair, her fingers white from the pressure they exerted on the tabletop, her eyes smoldering.

Leyla was close now; her eyes passed over me, then came back. I stared into them; the intelligence in their brown depths blended nicely with an uninhibited sensuality. Together, the two elements made a heady brew. She was an artist who spoke with her body, and that was something I could appreciate.

It wasn't likely she'd forget the only dwarf in the place, but I wanted to make sure. I reached into my wallet, fished out a twenty. Leyla removed the other bills from the cleft and bent over, momentarily exposing the topography of her breasts. I slipped the twenty into the inviting space and stared after it. Her brown, taut nipples were surprisingly dry, dancing to a beat of their own on the rounded surfaces of her breasts. I quickly looked away; the musky odor of her hot body was in my nostrils, and I gulped at my drink as Leyla returned to the center of the dance floor, finished her dance in a wild, blurred spin, then crumpled into an exhausted mound of slippery flesh. I applauded with the others, clapping until my hands hurt.

"How did you find out about this place?" Bannon asked as the roar of the crowd subsided.

"It was recommended. Actually, I came here looking for a certain Iranian."

It seemed to me that Bannon's clapping hands missed a beat, but that could have been my imagination. Gradually the last beats of applause faded away and the waiters started their rounds. Leyla, still breathing hard, rose from the floor and disappeared through the curtain. I stole a glance at Bannon's wife; she seemed almost as exhausted as the dancer. Her hands were trembling as she reached for her drink.

"This Iranian you're looking for," Bannon said, turning toward me. "A friend?"

"No. I'm working for a client. I'm also a private investigator."

"You didn't mention that you were a detective," he said tightly, quickly looking away. "It must be an interesting line of work."

"It can be."

"Then it was no accident that you came over by our table?"

"You're American, Mr. Bannon. You speak English, and you looked like a regular. I thought you might be able to help."

Bannon's thick, stubby fingers flexed, and his right hand closed around his glass. He didn't drink, and he didn't look at me. "You should talk to Leyla. She sees everyone who comes in here."

"Thank you. I was thinking of doing just that. In the meantime, I thought you might have seen him."

Bannon glanced quickly at the photograph I showed him, then shoved it back at me. I thought his movement was just a bit too quick, too tense. "I haven't seen him," Bannon said shortly. "Besides, the chances are slim that he'd show up here."

"Really? What makes you say that?"

Bannon swallowed hard, and the worms of muscle in his jaw worked rapidly. "Why should he come here? The Santur isn't very well known."

He was lying, and I felt my pulse quicken. "Well, maybe your wife will recognize him."

When I started to lean across to Soussan Bannon, her husband made a sudden move, knocking over his water glass, drenching my hand and the photograph; it hadn't been an accident. The florid-faced man shoved my hand away and forcefully dabbed with his napkin at the spreading blotch of water. Finally he signaled the waiter, who hurried over and assumed the job of mopping up.

A number of people had turned to stare at us. Soussan's face was flushed. She started to speak to me, but her husband interrupted, speaking sharply to her in Farsi. She tensed and quickly looked away.

Bannon turned to me. "We came here to enjoy ourselves, Frederickson," he said, "not to spend an evening answering silly questions from a dwarf pretending to be a private detective!"

It was ugly, and loud enough for most of the people in the dining area to hear. There was a sudden rush of whispers and tittering laughter. Bannon was trying hard to embarrass me; he had no way of knowing that these laughers were amateurs compared with some of the rubes who'd filled the circus stands. I sat quietly while the band hurried back to the stage and started to play. Bannon turned his back to me and began talking earnestly with his wife while I sipped my watery Scotch and studied the band. I'd left the photograph on the table in front of me, but Soussan Bannon studiously avoided even glancing at it. Half a minute later, Bannon announced, loudly enough for me to hear, that he was going to the men's room. He rose and headed toward the rear, veering away at the last moment and slipping through the green curtain.

I picked up the photograph and held it in front of the woman's face. "Mrs. Bannon, I wonder if I might—"

"I'm sorry, Mr. Frederickson," she said, her voice barely audible. Her hands were clenched tightly together and she was staring intently at the tablecloth in front of her. "My husband has asked me not to speak with you further. You are spoiling our evening with your questions."

"That's obvious," I said evenly, putting the picture back into my pocket. "I'm sorry if I've offended you."

She remained silent, avoiding my eyes. I turned back to the front. A few minutes later, Bannon emerged through the folds in the heavy curtain and returned to the table. He spoke a few words to his wife. She rose, clutching her purse tightly, and moved away. Then Bannon turned to me.

"I'd like to apologize, Frederickson," Bannon said, his face a relaxed, fleshy blank. "It's my work: I've been under a lot of pressure. I realize you're just doing your job, and I'm very sorry I lost my temper. I'm also sorry I couldn't be of any help. I wish you luck."

He went after his wife, who was standing across the room by the exit. I watched them leave, then moved across the crowded dance floor and through the green curtain. There was a narrow, dingy corridor on the other side, with toilets at the end. To my right was a door with a crack of light showing under it. I knocked, and Leyla's voice answered.

"Bale?"

Taking that as an invitation, I went in. Leyla was sitting on a wicker chair sipping a Coke. She'd rubbed herself down with a damp towel and her body gleamed like wet brown marble. On the table next to her was a pile of paper money. One of the bills was a hundred, which meant that someone either was a true patron of the arts, couldn't read zeros or was willing to pay a premium for special service, like silence.

"My name's Frederickson," I said. "I'd like to ask you some questions." Leyla shook her head as though she didn't understand. Her eyes were very dark, unblinking, as she stared at me. I showed her the photograph of Khordad. "Have you ever seen this man before?" Leyla shook her head, and I acted it out. She looked at the photo, shrugged, then handed

51

it back to me. I pointed to the hundred-dollar bill on the table; it was crisp and dry, unlike its soggy companions. "Bannon?" I asked. Still pointing to the bill, I stepped closer to the table. "Did Mr. Bannon give you this money not to talk to me?"

Leyla laughed pleasantly, reached out and shoved the money into a drawer. What she did next was totally unexpected; she reached behind her back and undid her halter clasp. Her full breasts fell out across her chest, quivering. Slowly she removed the halter, tossed it on the table and stood up, her arms at her sides and her chest thrust forward. Her nipples were hard and pointing directly at me. The muscles in her belly fluttered as she hooked her fingers into the top of her silk trousers, then stepped out of them to reveal a large thatch of moist pubic hair.

It wasn't money she was after. I knew where she was coming from, because she was the latest in a long, jaded line. I recognized the peculiar breathlessness, the electric aura of anticipation. Leyla was curious; she wanted to see if I was dwarf all over.

But I wasn't in the mood for a demonstration. Like my other, more public performances, the demonstrations, over the years, had been too many, and they were part of a past I was trying to forget. I dropped my card and a copy of the photo on her dressing table.

"Very kinky," I said, "but my love life always suffers when I've got questions on my mind. I think you can understand me. If you do see this man, I'd appreciate a call." I walked to the door, then turned and grinned. "I can't afford your prices, but if you do remember something I'll reward you with my body."

Leyla's smile flickered, then worked it was across her face. It was a pleasant smile which she tried hard to stop and couldn't. Finally she broke out laughing. "I'll call you if I see him," she said in perfect English.

"Call me anyway."

"I may do that," she said, still laughing. I stepped out into the corridor and closed the door behind me.

Out on the sidewalk I gulped the cool night air. Suddenly I was very tired, the inside of my head swollen with too much Scotch and too many unanswered questions. My watch read three o'clock in the morning. I jotted down a memo of my conversation with Orrin Bannon, then hailed a taxi. I gave the driver my address, then settled back in the seat to stare out at the deserted streets. A light rain had begun to fall.

4

THE ALARM HAD BEEN SET for seven, but I woke up fifteen minutes early with a clear head and no apparent aftereffects from the night before. It meant I was into the case, excited. I'd pay for the lack of sleep later, but at the moment I was anxious to get going; I had a lot of checking to do. But first it was bread-and-butter time. I studied my lecture notes for an hour over coffee and toast, then went to the university for my ten-o'clock class.

Ali Azad was waiting for me when I finished. He hadn't shaved, and his jaw and cheeks around his moustache looked as if someone had sketched them in with a piece of charcoal. I wasn't happy to see him; for now, the best lead I had was a nervous, big-spending American, and I wasn't anxious to be delayed by a paranoid Persian. On the other hand, I couldn't afford to cut off any source of potential help.

"I'd like to speak with you, Dr. Frederickson." Azad's manner was still tense, but the hostility and suspicion were missing from his voice.

"All right, I'm listening. But I need coffee."

We went down to the Student Commons in the basement, where I bought coffee and Azad took tea. We went over to a corner table warm with the morning sun pouring in through an open window. He seemed to be having a hard time getting started, and after the episode in his office I wasn't anxious to help. I let him stare into his tea while I lighted a cigarette.

"You really *were* looking for this man, Hassan Khordad," he said at last. He sounded vaguely surprised.

"Congratulations. What finally convinced you?"

"One of our members followed you to The Santur last night. He heard you asking questions about Khordad."

"I don't like being followed, Ali," I said evenly.

"We had to make certain you are who you say you are."

"For Christ's sake, Ali, I've been teaching here for more than five years."

He bared his teeth in a grimace that might have started out as a smile. "You think I'm paranoid, Dr. Frederickson. Just remember the saying that even paranoids sometimes have real enemies."

"Who are your enemies?"

"My government, and your government. The Confederation of Iranian Students is considered a threat to the stability of the Iranian Government." He lifted his cup and stared at me over the rim. "Also, the Shah doesn't like criticism. What the Shah dislikes, the United States Government also dislikes."

"No offense, Ali, but any threat posed by your organization to the Iranian Government seems to me to be rather, uh, piddling."

"We don't like to think so!" he snapped, white lines appearing at the corners of his mouth.

"What did you want to talk to me about, Ali?"

"The fact that we do not trust people easily is not as strange as you may think. We *are* watched; the SAVAK

55

photographs us constantly, and our telephones are tapped."

"The SAVAK: that would be the Iranian secret police."

"Correct."

"You say they're operating in this country?"

"Of *course* they're here," he said with a tight, wry smile. "Anywhere you find two Iranians, you can be certain one of them is probably SAVAK."

"I assume you're a legal resident of this country. If you feel you're being spied on, why don't you complain to the U.S. authorities?"

He looked at me strangely for a moment, then burst into an odd, hiccuping laugh that was razor-sharp with bitterness. "The *authorities*!" he yelped. "Oh, God, Dr. Frederickson, that is *funny*!"

"Ali, people are staring."

Suddenly he leaned forward, half-rising out of his chair. His breath, tinged with the smell of spice, hissed in my face. "Don't you think the U.S. authorities *know* the SAVAK operates here? The C.I.A. and the F.B.I. *help* them." He paused, apparently displeased by something he saw in my face, and sat back down in his chair. "You don't believe me?"

"C'mon, Ali, you're going to blow a blood vessel. I know the SAVAK is here; I read the papers. I'm just not sure how much help they get from us."

The desperate anger in him seemed to pass as quickly as it had come. His shoulders sagged and he sighed resignedly. "It doesn't matter," he said quietly. "You will find out for yourself if you continue to investigate this matter. In any case, I have decided to trust you."

"Gee, Ali, that's swell."

He missed or ignored the sarcasm. "I want to help you, Dr. Frederickson." He'd begun to talk very rapidly. "I can't tell you where your man is, but I can tell you *what* he is."

"I thought you already had: he's a nasty refugee jock from some Iranian gym."

"There's more. I said he was an assassin, but I didn't tell you why I was so sure. And I *am* sure. I'm also sure I know *whom* he came here to kill." His voice grew softer, then broke, as if he were choking on his words. "I believe he may already have succeeded, and that's why you can't find him."

"Let's back up a minute, Ali. Khordad's been with an American circus for two years, and the last time we spoke you hadn't even heard of him."

"I don't have to know him personally to know what he is; he is SAVAK. If he were not, he would have no interest whatsoever in joining an American circus. You simply must be made to understand that. Hassan Khordad's only purpose in coming here was to take care of some kind of business for the Shah. Sincere members of the *Zur-khaneh* are interested only in developing the body, mind and spirit; they care nothing for circuses." He paused, drummed his fingers on the table. "Just last month an anti-Shah general was assassinated in Iraq by a group of SAVAK agents. Check it out if you don't believe me."

"And you claim the Shah ordered that?"

"Of course not. The Shah doesn't order any of these things, any more than your President personally gives orders to an individual C.I.A. agent. It just isn't done that way."

"Who gives the orders in Iran?"

"The head of the SAVAK is a man by the name of Bahman Arsenjani. Arsenjani is very powerful; he comes from a family that is famous for producing SAVAK personnel. Indeed, it's rumored that he uses members of his family to spy on other SAVAK agents. It is Arsenjani's job to anticipate the wishes of the Shah. If Bahman Arsenjani thinks that the Shah would be made happy by somebody's death, Arsenjani will see to it that the individual is killed. Arsenjani is ruthless, and he has a completely free hand. He will go to great lengths to search out and destroy the Shah's enemies, wherever they may be. Perhaps now you'll understand why I believe that Hassan Khordad was sent here to kill an enemy of the Shah, and that the circus was only a . . . a . . . what do you call it?"

"We call it a cover. Whom would Khordad want to kill?"

"Mehdi Zahedi. Mehdi is the president of our chapter, as well as president of the national organization. He is a student here."

It was the name Anna had spoken over the telephone. It still sounded familiar and I still couldn't place it. I said so.

"Mehdi is a postdoctoral economics fellow," Ali said. "But this year he has been away from the campus a great deal. He is a wonderful speaker and is very good at organizing demonstrations. That is what he has been doing."

"Speaking and organizing against the Shah?"

"Of course. He began receiving national attention around December."

"When does he find time to study?"

"He studies," Ali said with a shrug. "He is a genius; as far as I know, he's never failed an examination. I'm surprised you haven't heard of him. There was a long article on him in *The New York Times*."

"When?"

"Sometime in January."

That explained it; I'd spent the entire month of January holed up in an experimental crime lab. "Go on," I said.

Ali whispered something I couldn't make out. I leaned forward and asked him to repeat it.

"GEM," he said, quickly glancing over his shoulder. "The Shah may deny that it exists, but we know—"

"Hold it, Ali. I don't know what you're talking about."

He swallowed hard, and I watched as his eyes grew wide and very bright with excitement. His voice was still barely above a whisper, but it hummed with passion. "There is an

organization in Iran we call the *Grouhe Enghelaby Makhfi*
—'secret revolutionary group.' They have had that bastard
Shah chasing his tail for years; GEM has become a legend.
Twice, it is rumored, they almost killed the Shah. Soon—
Allah be with us—they will succeed. The Shah and SAVAK
deny that GEM even exists, but we all know better."

"Did Zahedi belong to GEM?"

Ali sadly shook his head. "If Mehdi had been GEM, he
wouldn't have been here. No one knows who belongs to
GEM. I . . . I would gladly trade the rest of my life for the
chance to serve just one year with GEM . . . if only they
would ask me." Incredibly, there were tears in his eyes. He
quickly wiped them away with the back of his hand. "But
the way must be prepared. The new John Foster Dulleses of
this world must know that Iran can be free without posing
any threat to them. *Your* government, your *people*, must be
prepared for the death of the Shah and the coming revolution
in Iran. That is what Mehdi had been doing so well. Mehdi
was speaking, and people were listening. That is why he was
so dangerous to the Shah." Ali paused and stared directly
into my eyes. "Mehdi has been missing since February
twenty-second. I don't believe it is a coincidence that your
man is missing too; Hassan Khordad was almost certainly
sent here to assassinate Mehdi."

"Khordad was here a long time before Zahedi surfaced," I
said. "Besides, the dates are wrong. Khordad left the circus
on March fifteenth. That's three weeks *after* your president
turned up missing."

Ali was studying the palms of his hands. "I can't explain
that; I just know what I feel in my stomach. It is enough
that both of them have disappeared."

"You think the Shah really considered Mehdi Zahedi that
much of a threat to him?"

"Yes!" Ali said, his eyes and voice heating up again. "Our
struggle can succeed only if the United States stays out of it.

Don't underestimate the role public relations plays in modern-day revolutions."

"That's not exactly Maoist thinking."

"It's realistic thinking. The Confederation, with Mehdi as our spokesman, has been acting as the unofficial propaganda arm of GEM. In view of recent Iranian history, it is *vitally* important that the United States Government be persuaded that its interests will not be harmed by a revolution in Iran. Nothing else can be accomplished until that basic step is taken."

Ali swallowed the rest of his tea in a single gulp, then wrapped his hand around the cup so hard I was afraid it would shatter. I moved my chair back a foot. "In the view of your government," he continued, "the Shah represents stability in the only Middle East nation, except for Israel, uncompromisingly friendly to the United States. Never mind the fact that Iran is a total police state. The Shah spends millions of dollars a year polishing his image. What we needed was a spokesman who could effectively present the truth about that pig Pahlavi to the American people. The fact that people—important people—were starting to listen to Mehdi was sufficient reason for him to be killed."

"All right; you had an Iranian Alexander Solzhenitsyn."

"Exactly, GEM, when it is able to surface and fight openly, must be seen as a group of freedom fighters, the hope for Iran's future. Mehdi was able to drive that point home. At this very moment there are thousands of political prisoners rotting in Iranian jails. Some are tortured so badly they can't walk, talk, piss or shit; they die in the poisons generated by their own bodies! If we can make the American public aware of this, *they* will make it very embarrassing for this government to interfere in our revolution."

"Who finances you?"

"I won't tell you that. I will say only that much of the money comes from Iranians living in the United States. They are men opposed to the Shah who feel, for one reason or another, that they can't be quite so outspoken."

"That's called hedging your bets."

"Of course. But it makes no difference to us; we'll take anyone's money."

"When did Zahedi begin all this activity?"

"He's been in the graduate school a year and a half, and he's been politically active since the day he arrived."

"Where'd he come from?"

"Iran. Tehran University. He left when he realized he could no longer tolerate seeing his country raped by the Shah."

"Why did the Iranian Government let him out in the first place?"

"Mehdi hadn't been politically active in Iran. He realized it would be useless to try to raise his voice in a country where he would be thrown into prison five minutes after he opened his mouth. Originally he simply planned to leave. It wasn't until he got here that he realized he had special gifts of leadership which could contribute something to GEM's cause. He quickly rose to the presidency of our local chapter, and was elected national president six months after that."

"Still," I said, "Khordad was here before your president started his political number. Unless this Bahman Arsenjani is psychic, it wouldn't make any sense for him to bury an agent in a circus while he was waiting for Zahedi to get his act together." Actually, I was in no position to discount any possibility, especially in view of the fact that Khordad had almost certainly had a contact at the university; that contact could have fingered Zahedi, marked him as a target. But Ali was more than a little excitable, and I wanted to make sure I had all my facts straight before I started drawing any conclusions.

Ali's face was flushed. "I'm not saying Khordad was *originally* sent here with a specific order to kill Mehdi. I am only saying he was sent here on the Shah's business, and that business *became* the killing of Mehdi. If you don't want to believe me, that's your business."

"It's not a question of belief, Ali. It's a matter of making all the pieces fit." One problem was Khordad's behavior. Governments don't send amateurs out to bring off assassinations on foreign soil; disappearing and leaving all your belongings behind was definitely sloppy and just didn't match Ali's fantasy of a cold-blooded, professional agent.

Ali had begun to sulk. He was beating a nervous tattoo on the tabletop with a long, manicured fingernail. "The pieces will fit, Dr. Frederickson. But Mehdi is one of those pieces; you can't solve your puzzle without him."

"All right, let's go over it again. Your president just vanished on February twenty-second."

"He didn't exactly 'vanish.'"

"What, then?"

Azad thought for a moment. "He received a call that morning at the Confederation office. I was there when it came in."

"He must have received lots of calls."

"Yes, but they didn't usually upset him."

"This one did?"

"Yes. He told me he had to go to Washington that evening for a meeting with some Congressmen. He said he'd be gone three days."

"And when he didn't return, you notified the police?"

"Yes. They were *very* polite about it," Ali said, sarcasm bleeding into the bitterness in his voice. "They said they'd *certainly* let us know if they turned up anything on him."

"I take it you didn't believe them."

"If Mehdi was murdered in this country by the SAVAK, your government will make certain nothing is done about it."

"You really believe that?"

Ali stared at me for a long time, then said quietly, "It is a fact."

I decided to change the subject. "So, the gist of all this is that you'd like me to let you know if *I* turn up anything on Zahedi while I'm looking for Khordad?"

"Yes and no."

"Give me the no part first."

"We will not ask you to work for us without payment."

"That's not important; I already have a client. I'll let you know if I find out anything. What's the yes part?"

"We knew we couldn't count on the police, so we used some of our money to hire our own private detective. He came highly recommended. Two days after we hired him, he called and told me he thought he had a good lead."

"Did he say what it was?"

"No, and we haven't heard from him for over a week. There's no answer at either his home or his office; I was hoping you might know him, or know where to find him. His name is John Simpson."

5

THE CONFEDERATION OF IRANIAN STUDENTS was out one private investigator, and I had a case that was growing tentacles. That was what I told Garth.

My brother listened to me patiently, then went and got the latest computer printout from Missing Persons. "Nothing's turned up on your man," he said, scanning the file. "Have you checked out the hospitals?"

"Not yet. I came to find out if they'd done an autopsy on John Simpson."

Garth looked up. "Of course. Why?"

"I take it he didn't fall into the East River by himself."

"Somebody cracked his back for him. They found bruises around the spine."

"Lovely. What have you got on him?"

"Well, he'd never had his license suspended, which makes him exceptional right away. He enjoyed a good reputation. Had a lot of girlfriends, but lived by himself. He ran a strictly one-man operation. He's got some family out in Nevada. They're coming in to get the body and arrange for his personal effects."

"Where was his office?"

"He used a small brownstone in the East Forties for both home and business. We've got it sealed off until the D.A.'s office has had a chance to look over everything."

"How long is that going to take?"

"How the hell should I know, brother? I'm not even assigned to the case."

"You sound a trifle irritable. I thought Neptune had totally mellowed you out."

"My love life's fine. It's too many goddamned reports."

"Isn't that unusual?"

"Too many reports?"

I slapped him hard on the stomach. "*Simpson*, you dummy! I mean, it's been a few days now since he was murdered. When his family gets here, I'd think you'd want to show them more than a sealed office."

"C'mon, Mongo, you know the statistics; the two things New York has piles of are dog shit and dead bodies."

"But you know the difference."

"Damn right I do, and the N.Y.P.D. damn well doesn't need you to tell us how to do our job." Garth paused. I waited. "Sorry, Mongo," he continued quietly. "It *is* those damn reports; I see more papers than I do people."

"Can you get me into Simpson's office?"

"Is there really a Santa Claus? I told you it's sealed. The D.A. would have your license and my job."

"Okay. What did Simpson have on him when you made the I.D.?"

"A few laminated cards that the water didn't get to. One of them had his name and address."

"Will you let me see his file?"

"My God, you *do* believe in Santa Claus. The last file I showed you concerned our old friend Victor Rafferty. Before you could say 'Mongo the Magnificent' we had bodies piled up all over the place, intelligence agents from four countries climbing up each other's backs, and *you* strung up, cut up and damn near electrocuted. You *do* remember Kaznakov?"

"I remember Kaznakov," I said quietly.

"Well, I ended up with everyone up to and including the Commissioner stomping all over *me*. They *still* haven't forgotten the Rafferty thing. And you want me to show you a *file?*"

"C'mon, Garth," I said with a shrug and a grin. "That was more than a year ago. I'm sure I'm universally beloved once again. There just may be a tie-in between my case and your dead detective. Hassan Khordad had a contact at the university, probably an Iranian. This Mehdi Zahedi I told you about disappears, then Khordad disappears. Simpson is hired to find Zahedi and he winds up with a broken back."

"Interesting," Garth said as though he really didn't think it was. "Aside from the fact that Zahedi and Khordad are both Iranian, where's the connection?"

"Uh, it takes a strong man to break another man's back with his bare hands?"

Garth groaned. "Pun intended?"

"If you like."

"So you think this missing student may have been Khordad's contact?"

"Not likely. From what I understand, they were at opposite ends of the political spectrum."

"Then you don't think they eloped?"

I could understand Garth's skepticism; I now found myself with the dubious distinction of defending a theory I'd dismissed the day before as rank paranoia. "Khordad is an assassin; Zahedi was his intended victim."

"Fifteen minutes ago you told me Khordad disappeared three weeks *after* Zahedi."

"Maybe Zahedi took off because he was warned."

"By whom?"

"How the hell do I know? Hey, I didn't say I was preaching the Gospel. But I've given *you* some information, and I think it would be nice if you did the same for me."

Garth laughed. "*What* information have you given me? All I've heard is a theory."

"Now you know whom Simpson was working for and whom he was looking for when he was killed. That should be worth a peek at his file."

Garth drummed his fingers on the desk for a few moments, then abruptly stood up. "You're right. And what you say about the possible link makes sense. I'll see that it's looked into." He paused, laughed again. "I *know* I'm going to regret this. I can't wait for the phone to start ringing." He stepped out of his office, then returned in a few minutes with the file on John Simpson.

Everything Simpson had been carrying with him was in the file, but most of it was gray mush; a set of keys and a few laminated cards were the only items that had survived the immersion in the East River. There were the usual host of credit cards, a laminated Social Security card and two plastic business cards: Simpson's card and that of an import-export company on the East Side. Everything that was paper was illegible. I copied what I needed from the report. "Did he carry a gun?"

"He was wearing an empty shou'der holster when we fished him out."

"You did say somebody had at least taken a look inside the office before it was sealed?"

"Right. From what they tell me, he was a great filer. We just didn't have the manpower to sort through everything."

"And that's exactly why I want to take a look at what's there. Remember, whoever searched through there before didn't know what Simpson was working on; they wouldn't have known what to look for."

"Sorry, Mongo. That brownstone's off limits."

"Well," I said, rising, "I certainly wouldn't want to get in bad with the New York City Police Department."

"Damn straight, brother. Try not to get caught."

It took me forty-five minutes to work my way through the police lock they'd put on the door. By then I was running short on time; it was getting dark, and I couldn't risk lights.

I went for the filing cabinets first. It was only then that I realized Garth had been practicing some of his subtle sarcasm when he'd described Simpson as a great filer; Simpson had apparently filed literally everything he could get his hands on, then promptly forgotten about it. The files were a paper jungle.

Such people didn't usually put things they wanted to lay their hands on in their files, but I went through Simpson's anyway. In the bottom drawer of one cabinet I found a folder marked with the initials M.Z. I sat down at Simpson's desk and began looking through it. Checking the files on Mehdi Zahedi quickly turned out to be tedious work; it was obvious most of the information in the file had come from Ali Azad, and Ali had been very thorough, giving Simpson a volume of information on Zahedi's public activities, habits and life-style; but it struck me that there seemed to be very little on Zahedi's personal life. Zahedi the man was completely overshadowed by Zahedi the political activist. I would have loved to find the name of a woman, but there wasn't any.

In the back of the folder was a small, ten-cent spiral notebook filled with scribbled notes that were mostly illegible and looked old. It was beginning to look as if John Simpson had kept most of his notes in his head—in which case the lead he'd mentioned to Ali had died with him.

Toward the back of the notebook I found one page

marked with Zahedi's initials again, and underlined; the notebook had apparently changed files a good many times. At the bottom of the page was a phone number. I picked up the phone on his desk and got a dial tone. I dialed the number and a lilting, professionally trained woman's voice came on at the other end.

"Good evening. Iran Air. May I help you?"

No. Not yet, at any rate. I hung up the phone and started through the Zahedi file again. This time I had a little better idea of what to look for, and I found it folded into another set of papers that had been stapled together. The sheet was a photocopy of the first-class passenger list for Flight 19, New York to Tehran. There were twelve names on the list, and Mehdi Zahedi wasn't one of them. However, Simpson had circled one of the names in red ink: Nasser Razvan.

Flight 19 had left John F. Kennedy Airport on the evening of February 22—the same day Mehdi Zahedi had disappeared.

When I called the office of the Confederation of Iranian Students, I got Anna. She got Ali.

"Ali," I said, "what would happen to your boy if he decided to go back to Iran?"

"You're joking, of course."

"I'll let you know when I'm joking. What I am is in a hurry."

"It would be *suicide*," he said after a slight pause. "Iran is a death trap for Mehdi. At the very least he would spend the next twenty years rotting in prison."

"Then you don't think he would have taken a first-class seat on Iran Air to Tehran?"

"It would be madness."

"Maybe he went under an assumed name."

"Impossible. The SAVAK checks and double-checks all papers."

"Does the name Nasser Razvan mean anything to you?"

"No," Ali said after a moment. "It is an Iranian name, but I've never heard of him. Who is he?"

"I don't know. I think Simpson found out, and it cost him his life. Now, did any *other* Iranian at the university drop out of sight in February?"

"No."

"It's a big campus."

"Yes, but there aren't that many Iranians here, and I know every one of them. Mehdi is the only one who is missing. I don't understand what you're getting at."

"Someone calling himself Nasser Razvan left New York for Tehran on the night of February twenty-second. Simpson thought it was important. Nasser Razvan may not have been his real name, and it wasn't Hassan Khordad, because Khordad was with the circus at the time."

"It wasn't Mehdi; it couldn't have been."

"But there could be some connection. Simpson obviously thought so."

"I don't see how there could be." Ali's voice was digging its heels into my ear.

"I need a few things from you," I said curtly. "For openers, I want a complete list of your membership and an indication of how long each member has been at the university."

"Why?" The old suspicion was back, humming like a hot wire on a summer day.

"Because it's possible one of them is an informer. I remember what you said about half of every Iranian twosome being SAVAK."

"I wasn't talking about *us*!"

"Start considering that possibility."

"I don't believe it!"

"Just bring me the list," I said wearily. "If you're nervous about advertising your membership, remember that the C.I.A., the F.B.I. and the SAVAK probably have it anyway.

That's if *you're* to be believed. Also, I need a good picture of Zahedi. On second thought, don't bring them: I'll be by in half an hour to pick them up. Okay?"

"Yes," Ali said after a long pause. "I will do as you ask."

When I dropped by the C.I.S. office Ali was waiting for me with the list and picture. I fended off his questions, then got back into my Volkswagen and drove out toward the airport. The expressway was jammed, and my stomach churned all the way out. I parked the car and headed into the Iran Air office, where I picked out the prettiest girl I could find and walked to her counter. She was blond, blue-eyed, probably Scandinavian, with an Italian bustline and a French mouth. She was also close to six feet tall. I walked past the ticket counter and stood in the open area by the baggage scales.

"Can I help you, sir?" The mouth on the face of this magic mountain smiled, and I smiled back.

"I'd like to ask you a few questions," I said, leaning on the scale. "I'm a private investigator trying to locate a missing person."

The name tag on her uniform said Miss Larsson. Miss Larsson thought about it for a few moments, then nodded. The slight movement sent the golden hair rippling about her face like waves of liquid sunshine. "What would you like to know?"

I handed her the flight list I'd taken from Simpson's office. "First, I'd like to verify that this came from here."

Miss Larsson studied the paper. "Yes, it's one of our first-class passenger lists."

"From New York to Tehran on the night of February twenty-second?"

"That's correct."

"Were all these people definitely on that plane?"

"Not necessarily, Mr.—?"

"Frederickson. You, Miss Larsson, may call me Mongo."

Miss Larsson blinked rapidly; spots of color appeared high on her cheekbones. "Mr. Frederickson, this is only a preliminary list of the passengers originally scheduled for the flight. It's possible for someone to cancel at the last moment and still appear on that list."

She leaned forward to hand the list back to me and I caught a whiff of something that smelled like mountain flowers. "Can you tell me who made up this list, or who issued the tickets?"

"If the flight was direct to Tehran, Mike Carson probably handled it. I'll get him for you."

Miss Larsson made a call, and we spent the next few minutes discussing the fact that Miss Larsson was fascinated by private detectives because she'd learned English with the help of *Alfred Hitchcock's Mystery Magazine*. I was just beginning to regale her with tales of my own glorious deeds when Mike Carson arrived.

Carson was a young man, prematurely bald, with the kind of bullet head on which baldness is becoming. He'd just given up smoking; his right hand kept fluttering toward his empty shirt pocket, and the left side of his mouth was filled with Life Savers that had a tendency to click around his vowels. He was a busy assistant manager on his way up; I hoped he had a good memory. I showed him the list.

He looked at the paper and gave a perfunctory nod of his head. "You're the second man who's been here asking about this list."

I described Simpson.

"That's the guy; forty, forty-five years old, with a real eye for the women. He was checking out ass the whole time he was talking to me, but he never missed a thing I said."

"Did he have this list when he came to you?"

"No. That's what he wanted; he asked me for a copy of this specific list. I didn't see any reason not to give it to him.

I've got an eye for the women myself," he added, as though that explained his cooperation.

"He hadn't been in touch with you before that?"

"No. He just wanted the first-class flight list for Flight Nineteen. He seemed to know exactly what he was looking for."

"Who issued the tickets for that flight?"

"It could have been any one of a number of people. If you're looking for somebody in particular, your best bet would be to talk to the stewardesses. That was a while ago, so it's a long shot that anyone will remember, but they're trained to remember faces; good for business."

"Where can I find them?"

Carson thought about it a moment. "They're in Shiraz now; should be back in about a week. I can find out the exact date, if you want."

"No, that's all right. What about passports? They're checked here before takeoff, aren't they?"

"Right; along with the required vaccination certificates."

"How easy do you think it would be to fake an Iranian passport?"

"Any passport can be forged, but the Iranians are sticklers on the subject of passports. An Iranian can't get into or out of Iran with any *other* passport. And the passports have to be renewed every year at the consulate. It would be damn hard to get into Iran on a fake passport."

"What if an Iranian became a citizen of another country?"

He shook his head. "Iranians can't become citizens of another country; not if they want to go back to Iran. As far as their government is concerned, once an Iranian always an Iranian. They make no exceptions. If an Iranian tries to get into Iran with a foreign passport, he stays in Iran; it takes months to wade through all the red tape necessary to get out again."

73

"There must be *some* Iranians who've become American citizens. You mean they can't go back?"

"Only if they travel on an Iranian passport, and that's next to impossible to arrange."

"Somebody could still forge a *foreign* passport with a different place of birth, no?"

"Sure, except that a visa is required for entry into Iran. If the name and place of birth are fictitious, well, that individual's in trouble. The Iranian Government is very careful about who they let in. Even to get *out* requires an exit permit, and they check all records very carefully. Traveling to Iran on a fake passport—*any* fake passport—would be a risky business."

It looked as if I'd driven out to the airport for nothing. John Simpson had apparently lucked out in the beginning, stumbling over Nasser Razvan and knowing his true identity before he'd even asked for the flight list. But then, Simpson had ended up in the East River; I decided I'd rather be dry than lucky. I filled in a half hour showing Zahedi's picture to the various personnel at the ticket counters and drew a blank, as expected.

When I pulled out of the parking lot, the same brown, vinyl-topped Chevrolet that had followed me to the airport was behind me. The driver and the man with him weren't amateurs, but the peculiar vagaries of New York traffic dictated that they stay closer to me than they might in, say, Wabash. That meant no more than two or three cars to the rear, and I could catch glimpses of the car and the men in it when the traffic patterns behind me shifted or another car pulled by to pass.

It wouldn't have been hard to lose them, but I decided against it. For the moment, it was simply a matter of the blind leading the blind. Once they knew I was on to them, they'd be more careful the next time; I preferred knowing where they were. It was ten o'clock. I felt flat and stale, but there was one more stop I wanted to make: Madison Square Garden. I wanted to have another talk with Phil Statler.

By the time I got to the Garden, the Statler Brothers Circus was into its Grand Finale. I found Phil in the wings, studying every detail of the swirling, glittering panorama of animals and men.

"It looks good, Phil," I said, astonished to find that I felt a twinge of nostalgia.

"It'd look better if you were in there, Mongo," Phil said without looking at me. The nostalgia passed. "What have you got on Khordad?"

"He may be involved in some nasty business, like murder."

Now he looked at me. "I don't follow you."

"Khordad may have been running his own little sideshow while he was with you. There's a possibility he's an Iranian agent specializing in assassinations, planned and impromptu. I think the police are looking for him now with a little more enthusiasm."

The show was over. Elephants, tumblers, horses, clowns and jugglers made one last circuit around the arena and filed out at the north end. For some time I wasn't sure Phil had heard me above the din of applause, but when the last performer had filed out he turned and looked at me. His eyes were bright and hard. "Who'd he kill?"

"Maybe an Iranian graduate student, maybe a private detective, maybe no one."

"And maybe he was using my circus as a front?"

"It's a possibility. There are still lots of unanswered questions. The point is that this looks like more than just a Missing Persons case. If the police think so, they'll put men on it. That's why I have to know if you want me to stay with it. I'm costing you money."

Statler pulled on his cigar. "Stick with it another week at

least," he said after a pause. "I don't like being used."

"Fine. In that case, I want to take a look at what he left behind."

Statler took a key off a ring and jerked his thumb toward a large trailer that had been pulled in through the huge freight doors and parked alongside a rear wall. "It's in there. What isn't piled in the far corner is in the blue metal trunk on the left. Here's the key to the trailer; you'll have to figure out what to do with the lock on the trunk."

"Thanks, Phil. I'll manage."

Inside the trailer, I rummaged around until I found Khordad's blue trunk. It had a big lock of simple design, and I had it open in five minutes.

There were a few changes of clothing stacked in neat piles. I went through the pockets, then carefully inspected the lining of each item. Aside from a few Juicy Fruit gum wrappers, I found nothing. Khordad traveled light: two suits, some sport shirts, slacks and underwear, one extra pair of black shoes and three performing costumes. There were no personal items to speak of, except for a few trinkets and a stack of pornographic magazines he'd probably picked up on Forty-second Street on a previous visit to New York. It was strange; when a man carries the sum total of his life around in a trunk, there's usually more.

There was. In the bottom of the trunk, tucked into the folds of a new shirt, I found his passport. It was doubtful that Khordad would have had much success clearing up any visa problems without his passport; which meant he'd been lying about having trouble with the Immigration authorities. On the other hand, the presence of the passport indicated that he'd been telling the truth about planning to return in a few days; something had happened to change his plans.

His performing equipment and three pairs of worn weight lifter's shoes were piled in a corner of the trailer. I carefully checked through the items, but they were nothing more than what they seemed to be; they contained no clue as to who Khordad might really be, or where.

There was still too much missing; the trunk was just too neat. A circus performer accumulates odds and ends of himself, and these fragments of personality are usually scattered about the only home he knows for most of the year—his trailer or his locker. There were the trinkets and magazines in the trunk, but it wasn't enough. It was almost as if Hassan Khordad had been trained to leave as little of himself exposed as possible. I was convinced there had to be more, especially if he'd meant to return; the problem lay in finding it.

I emptied the trunk of its contents and tapped along the sides. They were solid, and so was the thick lid. When I tipped the trunk over, I finally found what I was looking for. The bottom was about two inches thicker than it should have been and sounded hollow when I tapped it. There was a beveled metal plate screwed on over the original bottom.

A screwdriver from the maintenance department took care of the plate, and a single nine-by-twelve manila envelope floated to the floor. I picked up the envelope and spilled the contents over the bottom of the empty trunk. There were a small notebook, a cheap scratch pad and an enlarged, glossy color photograph. The writing in the notebook was in what I could reasonably assume was Farsi, except for one English word that had been underlined several times: GEM. For the rest of it I'd need a translator, and I had someone in mind.

I put the notebook in my pocket and turned my attention to the photograph. It was a picture of the same ruins I'd first seen inside the office of the Confederation of Iranian Students; beautiful pillars of stone and rubble stretched out across a desert landscape.

However, there was a difference: Hassan Khordad's photo showed the skeleton of a huge wooden platform rising up from the center of the ruins in the middle of a large, open floor of stone. Someone—probably Khordad himself—had circled two areas of the scaffolding in red grease pencil.

After putting the trunk back in order, I put everything back into the envelope, tucked it under my arm and went looking for Statler again. He was in an office, relaxing with a cigar and a stein of dark German beer.

"You want a drink, Mongo?"

"I'd pass out."

"Did you find anything in that son-of-a-bitch's trunk?"

"Maybe. I want you to do me a favor." I handed him the envelope. "Seal this up good and mail it to me Special Delivery, care of the university."

"Sure. What's in it?"

"It could be Hassan Khordad's reason for being here, or his reason for leaving."

The night air felt good on my face and in my lungs. It hadn't been a completely unproductive day; I had a manila envelope that could conceivably lead me to Khordad, and, as if to reassure me that I was doing something right, I had two men following me.

The Chevrolet pulled up to the curb and both of them leaped out. They immediately moved to flank me, one to the front and the other to my rear. They had professional polish in the way they moved, but none of the other characteristics of the average hood; their eyes were clear and cold, but their faces were unmarked. They might have been twins; both looked in excellent shape, on the near side of forty, with suits—one blue and one brown—that had come off pipe racks. They looked very middle-class and very mean.

I had a license to carry a handgun, and I owned a Beretta which fitted nicely into a specially tailored shoulder holster. The problem was that both were home in the bottom of a drawer. The gun was a memento of a trip to Sicily, where I'd researched a series of monographs on the genealogy of a particularly nasty Mafia family. In Sicily the gun had felt good; back in the United States it had made me feel like the trailer for a B movie, so I'd put it away.

An older habit had been harder to break. I carried razors embedded in the toes of my shoes; illegal, but highly effective against anyone who might find a well-dressed dwarf a tempting target. Nasty, but essential. In my first year with the circus I'd almost been killed twice before I'd picked up on the razor business from other dwarfs. Also, I'd taken the trouble to learn virtually every nerve center and pressure point in the human body. That had given me a weapon, and the tumbling skills which I'd parlayed into a black belt in karate had given me a delivery system. I wasn't exactly defenseless. The problem was always determining just how much defense to use.

I watched the two men and waited for an opening. They were good, and they'd chosen a dimly lighted, deserted street where no one was likely to hear—much less pay attention to—any yelling I might do.

The blue-suited one in front was close enough so that I could see scalp shining through the close-cropped red hair on the sides of his head. I could sense the other, heavier man moving up behind me, cutting off my rear. I stood perfectly still and affected a moderately stupefied expression. The man in front of me began to relax.

"Get into the car, Frederickson," the redhead said. His voice was even, well modulated, like that of a man used to giving orders and having them obeyed. Like his partner, he seemed an odd choice for a run-of-the-mill pickup chore.

"But we haven't been introduced."

"Get in the car." He set his feet and motioned toward the curb.

It didn't seem like a good idea; I remembered the picture Garth had shown me of Simpson's puffed, blue face staring up at me from his stone bed in the morgue.

Neither man was showing a gun. I waited, listening to the big man's footsteps behind me. The smile on the redhead's face bordered on contempt, but my feelings weren't hurt; his contempt would give me the advantage of surprise.

The car, parked at the curb behind a truck, still had its motor running. I waited until the redhead reached for me; then I slipped under the man's outstretched arm and headed for the space between the car and the truck. But they had position. The man behind me grabbed my arm and spun me around. His partner recovered, then stepped forward and aimed a roundhouse right that glanced painfully off my shoulder.

Shifting my weight to my left leg, I lashed out with my right at the big man's kneecap. He grunted and went down with a surprised look on his face. I wheeled and drove the side of my hand into the redhead's thigh. But he was no slouch either; even as he clutched at his thigh with his right hand, his left bounced off my ribs. I spun again, absorbing the blow, driving my stiffened fingers into his side. He doubled over and I came up hard with my knee into his face. I felt his cheekbone crack, and he went down to his knees. I tensed, ready to kick the razor in my shoe across his throat, but I held back. Had either man pulled a weapon on me from the beginning, I probably wouldn't have hesitated to kill. But they hadn't, and that slowed up my reflexes. I regretted the decision when it was too late. The redhead reached inside his coat; when his hand emerged it was holding a gun.

There was no chance of getting close to him again. I flipped backward, hit the sidewalk, leaped up onto the hood of the truck, rolled over and dropped down to the street on the other side. I could see the redhead's legs coming around the rear. I rolled under the truck and came up on the other side, behind him. He turned, but not fast enough. I locked my hands together and drove them hard into his back, above his right kidney. His gun clattered to the sidewalk. I picked it up and moved into a position from which I could cover the two of them. Both men stared, uncomprehending. The heavyset man was still on the sidewalk, clutching his shattered kneecap. His partner's face went from a greenish white to a reddish hue that almost matched his hair.

"Now *you* get in the car," I said, pointing the gun at the man's belly. "And put your buddy in with you. *Move!*"

The redhead hesitated, and I clicked the hammer of the gun back; the man helped his crippled partner to his feet.

"Put him in the front," I said. "You drive." I waited while he eased the other man into the passenger's side, then followed him with the gun while he walked around the car and slid in behind the wheel. I got into the back.

Now, with a cocked gun at the back of his head, the man took directions well. In ten minutes we were outside Garth's precinct station. Inside, Sergeant Harry Stans did a double take.

"Mongo!"

"Hello, Harry," I said. I pressed the barrel of the gun against the redhead's spine, and he helped his partner forward to the desk. "I'd like to prefer charges against my two friends here. Aggravated Assault and Battery will do for a start. While you're at it, I'd also like to find out who sicked them on me, and why."

"Sergeant," the redhead said, "I'd like to talk to you."

"Well," Harry drawled, "that's very encouraging. First I have to warn you that you have the right to remain silent."

Harry's voice droned on, a little too matter-of-fact for my taste. But then, I was a prejudiced party. Harry, with his perpetually razor-nicked face and pouched eyes, was only a year and a half away from retirement; he'd seen enough in his time so that the sight of a dwarf pushing around two slightly used thugs wasn't cause for any great excitement.

When Harry had finished, the redhead very carefully

reached inside his coat. I tensed, and Harry made a move for his gun. Using two fingers, the man slowly pulled a billfold from an inner pocket of his suit jacket and laid it on the desk in front of Harry.

"Will you look inside my wallet, please?" the man snapped impatiently. It annoyed me that his voice had lost none of its arrogant, commanding tone. "There's an identification card there. I think that will explain everything."

Harry reached out for the wallet, opened it. His face blanched.

"My name is Victor Lanning," the redhead continued. "My partner's name is Wendell Biggs. You can verify who we are by calling the number on that card."

Harry picked up the phone and dialed the number. He talked for several minutes. I could hear only his end of the conversation, and I didn't like it—especially when he got to the "Yessirs." He hung up and turned his attention back to me.

"You really screwed up this time, Mongo," Harry said, a slight tremor in his voice. He got down off his chair, came around to the other side of the desk and gently took the gun away from me. "These men are from Military Intelligence. Their boss wants you locked up."

6

My FIRST REACTION had been regret that I hadn't shot them both, and a night in jail did nothing to sweeten my disposition.

"Military Intelligence! How the fuck was I supposed to know they were Military Intelligence?"

Garth sighed and sat down on the bunk across from me. "They said they identified themselves."

"That's bullshit! Now, you tell me: why would I want to screw around with two Military Intelligence agents, bust one up, then top it off by marching them down to the fucking police station? Does that make any sense?"

"Nope," Garth said easily. "That's why I believe you. But it doesn't make any difference. They're not bringing any charges against you."

"Against *me*? I'm bringing charges against *them*!"

Garth stared at me for a long time, and when he spoke his voice was strained with the special tension of a cop's sense of reality. "You know better, Mongo. The night in the slammer was just to show you who's in charge. You won't get anywhere; they'll tie you up in red tape until you can't breathe."

"Garth, those bastards jumped me."

"They claim they made a mistake. Case of mistaken identity. You weren't who they thought you were."

"Sure," I said, choking on a mouthful of jailhouse coffee, "they thought I was the ghost of Frodo Baggins."

"Frodo who?"

"Forget it."

"You forget it. Drop it, Mongo."

"There's an international espionage ring run by dwarfs!"

"You're jabbering at the wrong guy, brother. Look, you're lucky you're getting out of this with a night in the can. You know what could happen to you if they *really* wanted to make a point."

"Yeah? Well, how's *this* for a point? I'm not leaving this cell until someone *does* bring charges. I want to find out why those guys were after me."

"You're not going to find out, and you *know* you're not going to find out. They want the whole matter dropped, and dropped it shall be."

Garth was sitting quietly, staring at the backs of his hands. My mind raced, trying to make the necessary connections. "Okay," I said at last, "let me tell you just what I think is going on. Now, they did *not* show me any identification, but that isn't really all that surprising; they must have an illegal bug in the C.I.S. office. They've got no business messing with a civilian, and they know it. They must have been on my case because of this Khordad thing. They'd been following me for a while, but they didn't move in until I made a stop at the circus. They were afraid I'd found something."

"Did you?"

"Are you asking me as my brother or as a cop?"

"Your brother is a cop."

"Well, I'll talk to my brother, because I think the cops have been doing a crappy job on this."

"Now you're talking about Simpson?"

"Right. *That's* homicide. Simpson's tied into this Khordad case; I know it. And you want me to believe the cops aren't going to assign *somebody* to dig into Simpson's death? Why isn't someone going over his office right now with a vacuum cleaner? Go look for yourself; everything's just sitting there."

"Do you have any idea how many major crimes there are in this city every day?"

"But at least the department could go through the *motions.* Simpson's files haven't even been removed. I think somebody gave the word to lay off the Simpson case; it's like what happened with Victor Rafferty."

"You were going to tell me what you found at the circus," Garth said evenly.

"Khordad's trunk had a false bottom. I found some papers in it, and those papers are what those two jokers from Military Intelligence were after. They had no intention of identifying themselves, because that would have given me some clue as to what they wanted and why they were on my tail. When I got the drop on them and brought them in here, it screwed up the whole deal. They had to tip their hand to get out, but they couldn't very well press charges without giving away the whole show."

"You mean an illegal bug?"

"I mean the admission that Washington is working hand in glove with a network of foreign agents, right here in the United States. How would it look if the story broke that the United States was helping the SAVAK carry out the assassination of an Iranian national?"

"What are you talking about, Mongo?"

"I think there's a connection between the disappearances of Khordad and Mehdi Zahedi. Khordad killed John Simpson, possibly because Simpson found out that Khordad had killed Zahedi. Those papers I found could supply the proof.

I'm going to have them translated; then I'll get copies to you."

"Don't bother," Garth said quietly.

That stopped me. "What the hell does that mean?"

"The case is closed as far as the N.Y.P.D. is concerned."

There was nothing apologetic in his tone; somehow, I felt there ought to be. "Why? The State Department and Pentagon getting nervous?"

"I honestly don't know," Garth said evenly. "I'm just telling you what I've been told. I did check personally with the Immigration people; Hassan Khordad has never had any difficulty with them. He's perfectly legal all the way. Oh, and by the way: I asked them to run a check on this Mehdi Zahedi. As far as Immigration is concerned, he doesn't even exist."

"No? Then who's this guy who's been running around making speeches for the past year?"

"Beats me. But one thing's certain: his name isn't Mehdi Zahedi. That name isn't in Immigration's files."

"You find that out and you're satisfied to let it go by?"

"Hey, nobody's letting anything go by. First, Immigration isn't our responsibility; the government does its job, and we do ours. Second, the visitors from Military Intelligence make it obvious that things are being handled at a higher level. They probably just don't want anybody botching things up."

"What you mean is that you're letting them pressure you off the case."

"Watch your mouth, Mongo," Garth said softly. "For Christ's sake, nobody's checking anything off, but espionage isn't our department either."

"Murder is."

"There's no proof yet that Khordad killed anyone. If there is a foreign espionage ring operating here, then I'm sure the government boys are taking care of business. I think you're just pissed off because we won't help you find Khordad."

"Garth, those government men were after *me*, and they were after me because I'm after Khordad."

"I don't know why those men wanted you, but I do know they're working for the *government*. Don't you believe they're working in the national interest?"

"Is that a rhetorical question?"

"No, it's not. What's your problem?"

"My problem is that I feel a bit put upon. Those two men not only tried to mug me, they made up a fool story about thinking I was someone else."

Garth considered it for a few moments, then said, "I don't blame you for being pissed off. If I thought there was something being covered up, I'd fight it—and you damn well know I would. So far, I have no reason to believe things aren't going through the proper channels."

"You haven't been talking to the people I've been talking to."

"Maybe not. But it still looks like government business, and if I were you I'd forget it." He smiled thinly. "Of course, you're not going to."

"I've got a client."

"Who wants you to dig up Hassan Khordad. Drop it, Mongo. It's bad business. One of two things is true: either the government wants to find Khordad too, in which case you're not needed and probably in the way; or the government *doesn't* want him found, which means you could be in a lot of trouble if you *do* find him. Either way you lose."

I stood up and walked to the cell door. "Am I free to go now?"

"Free as the proverbial bird, and let's hope you don't end up a turkey." Garth paused, then continued very seriously: "Get out of it, brother. Remember what happened with the Rafferty case? This smells just as bad. You're going to wind up with the dirty end of whatever stick they want to shove into you."

"Thanks, Garth. I've got a ten-o'clock class to make."

After picking up a buttered hard roll and a carton of coffee for breakfast, I went back to my office at the university, where I kept an electric razor. While I was sipping at the coffee and running the razor over my face, I checked with my answering service. Phil Statler had called. I dialed the number he'd left.

"Yeah?" He sounded sleepy.

"Phil, it's Mongo."

He woke up fast. "Listen, you move in some pretty fast company."

"What's happening?"

"I had some visitors last night. They banged in here past three o'clock in the morning. Can you imagine that? Three o'clock in the fucking *morning*?"

"I can imagine it. Who were they?" I was pretty sure I knew the answer, but I wanted to ask just for the record.

"Government agents."

"What department?"

"They didn't say, and I didn't ask. They flashed badges that looked pretty real; I wasn't about to argue with them. They looked mean." The line went silent for a few moments. When Phil spoke again his voice was deeper, more reflective. "You know, you hear about things like that and you tell yourself you wouldn't stand for it. Then it happens, and you fold up like an accordion."

"Yeah. What'd they want?"

"They wanted me to show them Khordad's stuff."

"Did you?"

"Sure. Why not? I took them back to the Garden and we used their master keys. They tore right through his things, and they found where you'd ripped the bottom off his trunk. I figured that's where you found the envelope."

"Did you get that in the mail to me?"

"Check. I mailed it right after you left."

"Did you tell them about it?"

"No. By that time I was awake enough to be mad, and I figured I'd lie about anything I thought I could get away with. They asked about you, and I told them what I figured they already knew."

"Did you tell them I was working for you?"

"No. Couldn't see that it was any of their business. Same with the papers. I told them I didn't have the slightest idea what you'd found, if anything."

"Well, I hope you don't regret it. It looks as if the government is interested in Khordad. If so, there could be big trouble for anybody they figure is getting in the way."

"I pay my taxes. Are *they* going to let me know if they find him?"

"Don't hold your breath."

"Okay, then what I said before still goes."

"I'm having a lot of sources of information cut off. I'm not sure what I can do in the rest of the week."

There was another long pause at the other end of the line, then: "Stick with it, Mongo."

"You've got it." I hung up, downed the rest of my coffee and went to my class.

I'd been running too long on adrenaline, and I was beginning to pay the price. Still, I pushed through the lecture on criminology, capping it off with the story of how their professor, within the past twenty-four hours, had broken into a cordoned apartment, resisted arrest by two Military Intelligence agents and spent the night in jail. They considered it a real knee-slapper and laughed uproariously.

After finishing the lecture, I went back to my office in time to meet the mailman. The envelope with the picture and Hassan Khordad's notebooks was in my slot. I'd placed the photograph Ali had given me of Mehdi Zahedi in with the other items; that was the one I now took out and studied.

The picture, a blowup of Zahedi taken during a large demonstration at which he had been speaking, was in black and white, and grainy. Whatever Mehdi Zahedi had, it didn't photograph; but then, charisma rarely does. There was certainly nothing commanding in his physical presence. Yet, to judge by the expressions on the faces of the listeners closest to him, Zahedi had charisma to spare.

I put Zahedi at about the same age as Ali—twenty-six or twenty-seven. But Zahedi was thinner, made to seem even more frail by clothes that didn't fit properly. His dark hair was thick and curly, cut short. In the picture he was leaning out over the edge of a raised platform, haranguing his audience. He seemed suspended in air, as if he might have plummeted to the ground a second after the picture was taken.

After replacing the picture in the envelope, I tucked the envelope under my arm and headed toward the Center for Middle Eastern Studies, where I hoped to find Darius Khayyam.

From the beginning, at least in my own mind, Darius' presence had hovered over the case like the ghost in *Hamlet*. Ali's remarks indicated that there was a great deal about Darius I didn't know, things that were deeply resented by most or maybe all of the Iranian students on campus. The question of Darius' supposed sins intrigued me all the more because he never spoke of Iran, outside the obvious curriculum requirements of his class. Also, as far as I knew, Darius had never returned to Iran since coming to the United States.

Still, to judge by what Ali had implied, Darius carried secrets about Iranian history and politics that were not to be found in the many textbooks he'd written. I might need to know a few of those secrets; the more I poked at the mystery of Hassan Khordad, the more it seemed his spoor converged with Mehdi Zahedi's, both trails winding back through the years, with the two men acting out roles that had been defined for them in the past.

The door to Darius' office was open. Inside, Darius was at his desk, reading and taking notes. The entire oak surface in front of him was covered with open books and professional journals, the pages heavily annotated in his own hand. His mind was a vast repository of information, making him the best instant resource I'd ever found on virtually any subject dealing with political science, history or geography.

Tall and large-boned, Darius had very poor coordination; even the simple acts of standing up and sitting were made to seem like complex calisthenics, as if his mind were too busy sorting facts and figures to pay much attention to the network of nerves and muscles that were also its responsibility. His full head of white hair lent him a somewhat imperious air, which was misleading; in fact, Darius was one of the most humble, gracious and approachable men I'd ever met. His dark eyes were set deep in a face that, despite his many years in the United States, still spoke of the desert. His nose was far too large for the rest of his features, which had a refined delicacy about them, as if Nature had relented after the nose and spent more time with the rest of his head. He always spoke softly, with a minimum of gesture, as though his thoughts had to be couched in the same spare style as the prose in his books.

Darius glanced up from his books and grinned as I knocked on the door and stepped in. "Mongo, my friend! It's been a while."

"Too long, Darius. How are you?"

"*Khubam*," Darius said, nodding his thick-maned head enthusiastically. "I'm very well. *Shoma?*"

"Terrific, except that I wish I knew more Farsi."

"Then we'll have to practice more."

"I'd like that." I cleared my throat and touched the envelope under my arm. "I'd like to ask you a favor."

"Ask away."

"First, what can you tell me about a secret terrorist organization in Iran called GEM?"

Darius leaned back in his chair and laughed easily. "Where did *you* hear about GEM?"

"A student."

He laughed again. "GEM is a fairy tale."

"There aren't any terrorists in Iran?"

He shrugged. "A few; mostly suicidal types. There's nothing organized. Unfortunately, all the good organizers in Iran work for the Shah. To hear the students here talk—whisper would be a better word—about it, the members of GEM are some kind of supermen. It's a joke. People who sit safely in this country bad-mouthing the Shah need to believe in heroes in Iran who are doing what the critics wish *they* had the courage to do. No, Mongo, GEM is a figment of some overheated imaginations; it's a product of wishful thinking."

"I know of at least one SAVAK agent who seems to believe in this particular fairy tale."

He frowned. "Who?"

"You'll see for yourself. I'd like to find out what these mean." I placed the envelope on the desk.

Darius opened the envelope and shook out the contents. He stared at the photograph of the ruins for some time, then leafed through the notebook. The way he'd placed his hand across his brow could have been a natural gesture, but it meant I couldn't see what emotions, if any, were playing across the surface of his face. It was a long time before he spoke.

"May I ask where you got this material?" There was an odd tone to his voice that I couldn't read.

"I've got a case involving a missing Iranian." I showed him

the picture of Hassan Khordad and the circus flyer. He studied both. "I'm looking for this man; I think the picture and that notebook may help me find him."

"I believe this man may be more than a simple circus performer," Darius said carefully.

"That seems to be the consensus."

"He's the agent you spoke of?" Darius was staring at me intently.

"Right. I've been picking up some information here and there."

"Then you have certainly been told that . . . such men . . . are strong and very cunning. If this man is missing, perhaps it's because he does not wish to be found."

"That's been suggested too."

"SAVAK agents—and this man *is* most certainly a SAVAK agent—are very dangerous, my friend."

"I don't have to bring him back alive—just find out where he is."

Darius' eyes kept returning to the photograph of the ruined city. "How can I help you?" he asked distantly.

"What are those ruins?"

"Takht-I-Jamshid."

I rolled that around in my brain, then tried it on my tongue. "Takht-I-Jamshid."

"That's the Persian name. In the West, it's known as Persepolis."

"I've seen another picture of it; in the office of the Confederation of Iranian Students."

"Yes. Persepolis is a national symbol. It was built as the capital of the Persian Empire, and sacked by Alexander the Great in 330 B.C. I have some literature on it which you may borrow if you like. You may find it interesting."

"Thanks; I will. What's the platform?"

"It's hard to tell. It could be construction for the art festival they have each year in Shiraz. It's sometimes held at the ruins."

"So I've been told."

"You sound as if you'd been spending time in the Iranian community."

"Some. Do you have any idea why this man might have drawn a circle around that particular section of the platform?"

Darius shrugged. "Maybe he was merely doodling. What did you say the man's name was?"

"Hassan Khordad." I showed him the photograph again. "You haven't seen him around here, have you?"

"No. Why do you assume a man like this would be seen here at the university?"

"I think he knew someone here."

"Really?" He sounded skeptical. "This man certainly wouldn't feel at home here, and I strongly doubt he'd find a friend."

I pointed to the notebook. "Can you tell me what Khordad wrote in that?"

Darius took a pencil and paper out of his desk, then opened Khordad's notebook and began to scan the pages. After a few minutes he stopped and nodded his head. "I see where he's written 'GEM.' "

"There's something written beside it. Can you make it out?"

"It's just letters, a number and a name: LS-180, and Firouz Maleki."

He wrote the information for me on a piece of paper, which I put in my pocket. "What about the rest of the notebook?"

He scanned a few more pages, closed the notebook and shook his head. "I'm sorry, Mongo, it's just gibberish; it makes no sense at all."

"A code?"

"Undoubtedly." The Iranian paused, cleared his throat, then added softly, "I repeat, my friend—this man could be very dangerous."

"Thanks, Darius. I'll bear that in mind." Any doubts I still had about Khordad's being a SAVAK agent were fast disappearing; apparently, I'd stumbled on his master code book. Khordad obviously thought that someone named Firouz Maleki was a GEM member. LS-180 could only refer to the new and highly experimental American automatic rifle which had a laser aiming mechanism. I had no idea how a terrorist group could get its hands on the gun—but then, if the latest crime intelligence reports were to be believed, the Mafia had it. One LS-180 would make a formidable assassination tool; a dozen or so would send a battalion running for cover. I could understand why the Shah was nervous.

Darius was absently studying the cover of the notebook. I watched him, wondering why he was so disliked by Ali and not sure I really wanted to know. "You seem to know quite a bit about these matters," I said quietly. "Experience?" It was the wrong thing to say. Darius dropped his eyes and folded his hands in silence. I pressed ahead anyway. "I've heard a lot about this Mehdi Zahedi, but you're an internationally known and respected scholar. I'd think that *you* would be a natural leader for Iranian exiles."

"I'm not in exile," Darius said quickly. "I'm an American citizen."

"But the Shah's people killed your sister, didn't they?"

Darius blinked slowly, and his eyes seemed to grow murky. "Is that the question of a friend, or a detective?"

"Both," I said, deciding it was useless to lie. "As a friend, I'm interested in your background, but I'd never pry into a part of your personal life you didn't want to talk about. As an investigator, I'd like to know why Ali Azad suspects you of being Hassan Khordad's contact here at the university."

"Ali said that?"

"I'm reading between the lines. He said no *student* here would have anything to do with Khordad. It would seem to me very peculiar that a man would work for the people who killed his sister, but I think that's precisely what Ali believes. I'd like to know why."

"Is this why you came to see me?"

"That's part of it, along with the translation. I'd also like your reaction to what I just told you."

"Ali Azad is a fool," Darius said evenly.

"And Mehdi Zahedi?"

"Zahedi is a bigger fool."

"Why?"

Darius was trying hard not to show it, but I could see that I'd opened a Pandora's box of emotions. He was becoming increasingly agitated, while at the same time withdrawing deeper into himself. "Those two young men are fools because they believe they can overthrow the Shah by violence," he continued in a hollow voice. "A revolution in Iran is the unlikeliest thing in the world; pure nonsense. First of all, the Shah's regime is supported lock, stock and barrel by the United States Government. Iran has our most modern weapons."

"They haven't helped us much in the oil situation; it's the Shah who's always bellowing for more money. Maybe the relationship is cooling."

Darius shook his head. "The Shah represents a consistently friendly government in the Middle East. He still has our support."

"Ali claims Zahedi was neutralizing that support."

Darius made a derisive gesture. "With *words*? More childish nonsense. Zahedi's a dreamer who doesn't even understand his own countrymen. He assumes that a democracy would be better for Iran than the Shah."

"And you don't?"

"I don't. In a way, I support the Shah. He taught me a

painful but valuable lesson; he showed me that democracy isn't for everyone. It won't work in Iran. The people there *need* someone to worship and tell them what to do. The fact that Iran *celebrated* twenty-five hundred years of monarchy would seem to prove my point."

"It was the Shah who celebrated, not the people," I said.

"It's the same thing."

"Your sister believed differently," I said softly, probing.

"Forgive me, but she too was a fool." Darius' voice was tight as a drumhead, dripping bitterness like acid from a cracked battery. "She made the mistake of believing in her own people. As I'm sure you've heard, she was killed for her social consciousness, burned to death in her cell after being repeatedly raped by the animals who work for the Shah. But in effect, she was killed by her own people."

"With some outside help."

"The counterrevolt was engineered by the C.I.A., it's true. But that's an even worse insult to a people. To take *foreign* money to betray your country, as the leaders of the phony counterrevolution did, is beneath contempt. In any case, I try not to give it much thought. I no longer have any association with Iran, except as a Professor of Middle Eastern Studies."

"You don't miss your country?"

"*This* is my country."

"I mean the land where you were born."

"No," he said with a perfunctory wave of his hand, "I don't miss Iran at all."

"But you left voluntarily?"

"Yes. I was never a political man. I wasn't then, and I'm certainly not now. It was my sister, Farah, who was the revolutionary. After her death, my life in Iran became unbearable. I sold all I had and came here." He shrugged. "End of story, my friend."

"Could you go back if you wanted to?"

"Of course. I don't *wish* to. It's also probably true that I could wield considerable influence against the Shah in academic circles. I don't wish to do that either. You see, I don't blame the *Shah* for the fall of Mossadegh. Pahlavi is—has become—a politician, and power is his lifeblood, his game. *I* blame the people who could not hold on to a great prize when it was given to them. That is why Mehdi and Ali find my position less than attractive; I simply do not *believe* in Iran."

He paused, smiled wryly. "Do you know what's happening in Iran at this very moment? They're fighting a cholera epidemic. I happen to know that because I have friends in the United Nations, but you'll never read it in the papers because Iran refuses to report its cases to the World Health Organization. So the disease continues to spread. The Iranians are too *proud* to admit they have cholera; it's that kind of chauvinistic, destructive pride which will always damage them."

Darius swallowed hard. Beads of perspiration had appeared on his forehead. A car backfired in the distance. "Mehdi and Ali are young and romantic," he continued quietly. "But talk is cheap. If they choose to fight, let them fight. As for me, I consider their actions a waste of time. They're right in assuming I would do nothing to help them. On the other hand, they're wrong in thinking I would work against them. I know nothing of this Hassan Khordad."

"Ali thinks Zahedi's speeches were beginning to have some effect in this country, inasmuch as they were generating support here for a revolution in Iran. What do you think?"

"You can't be serious. First of all, there *is* no revolutionary movement in Iran. They're deluded if they believe one man's hot air can offset the Shah's guns and the millions of dollars the Iranian Government spends each year on public relations. Politicians talk but, like Mao, they know that power comes from the barrel of a gun."

"Zahedi's hot air may have been resented enough to have him killed."

Darius looked at me strangely. "Why do you say that?"

"Zahedi himself has been missing since the last week in February. When Ali's group hired a private detective to find him, the detective got his back broken for his trouble."

Darius was flipping through the pages of Khordad's notebook again. It wasn't warm in the office, but I noticed that the edge of his collar was damp. "I still find it hard to believe that Mehdi would be taken seriously," Darius said tightly. "But then, revolution is not a game for children."

From the tone of Darius' voice, I suspected that Ali's contempt carried more sting than Darius cared to admit. "There's nothing else you can tell me?"

"I can only repeat myself," Darius said, suddenly fixing me hard with his eyes. "The best advice I can give you is to drop this matter immediately. Iranian politics is a rough, dirty business; whatever your client is paying you, it's not worth your life. A man like Hassan Khordad will kill you with no more thought than he would give to crossing the street. And he's protected by your own countrymen. Don't expect your murderer to be punished."

I felt a chill as I thought of John Simpson. It was true that nobody, with the exception of Phil Statler, seemed to want Khordad found, and that included the police. And Statler's reasons were strictly personal, considerations of honor and pride that many would argue belonged to another, more innocent age. I had a number of easy outs, but wasn't inclined to take any of them. I had a case. Rather, the case had me; a familiar, dark spider inside my psyche was weaving an insidious, invisible web spun from my own very special needs.

Darius rose and placed his hand on my shoulder. "No good can come of this, my friend. Believe me when I say the cards are stacked against you."

I thanked Darius for his concern and left. At my office I checked with my answering service and was told that Neptune had called and wanted me to call her back as soon as possible. There was also a hand-delivered letter from Walter Manning, the chairman of my department. It was typed on official university stationery, with a handwritten note at the top.

Dear Bob,
Problems. Here's a draft of a letter I'm supposed to send you.

> Dear Dr. Frederickson:
>
> It has been brought to my attention that you are dividing your time between your contracted teaching duties and your well-known nonacademic pursuits. Specifically, it has been reported to me that you are spending an inordinate amount of time as a private investigator. After careful consideration, the Chancellor and I must conclude that this type of activity is not conducive to the pursuit of academic excellence.
>
> I would appreciate it if you would call my secretary for an appointment at your earliest possible convenience to discuss this matter. In the meantime, may I take the liberty of suggesting that your chances for contract renewal would be enhanced if you were to devote full time to your teaching duties.

Sorry. What can I say?
                              Walt

I crumpled the letter and made the wastebasket on the first toss. I found it interesting that someone who wanted me off the case had taken the trouble to talk to the Chancellor. The power play had drifted down to Walt Manning. I dismissed the letter from my mind and called the number Neptune had left. She answered on the first ring.

"Hi, beautiful. It's Mongo."

"*Precious.* Where have you *been*? I've been worried about you."

"Never to worry, m'dear. Everyone who knows me will tell you I'm indestructible."

"*Lucky* is what Garth calls you. Listen, I can't understand how Garth could have let you spend a night in jail. He's a policeman, isn't he?"

I laughed. "He couldn't have gotten me out of that jam if he were the District Attorney."

"Well, I'm really interested in your investigation. I mean, here you're looking for an Iranian, and *I'm* Iranian. I'd like to help you in any way I can."

She'd called at a bad time; actually, it was a good time made bad by the fact that I was tempted. I cradled the receiver under my chin, took out my notebook and flipped open to the address I'd copied from the business card that had been found on John Simpson's body. It was the Iranian Import-Export Company, located in a commercial area on the Lower East Side. "Garth wouldn't like the drift of this conversation," I said.

"Garth won't *know* about this conversation. Come on, Precious."

"It's a heavy case, Neptune."

"But there must be *something* I can do that's safe. After all, I speak the language and you don't." She paused, and I was too slow to fill in the silence. "Come on," she continued urgently. "I can tell by your voice that you can use my help."

I drummed my fingers on the desk, then said, "I have to check out something calling itself the Iranian Import-Export Company. Give me an idea of something I can talk about besides rugs."

"I'll do better than that. I'll come with you."

"Uh-uh."

"Precious, there are *thousands* of things you could talk

101

about, but they'll know you're a phony in two minutes. I can talk all afternoon—and believe me, Iranians *love* to talk with other Iranians. You'll do much better with me along. Now, I'll expect you to pick me up in fifteen minutes. And if you don't, I'll be *very* upset. See you in a few minutes. Bye-bye."

7

I'D HAD NO INTENTION of picking up Neptune when I'd hung up the phone, but slightly less than a half hour later I was buzzing her apartment. For one thing, Neptune was a hard woman to say no to, and she was obviously intrigued by the disappearance of Hassan Khordad: none of which would have made any difference if not for the fact that she probably *could* be very helpful on this particular errand, and I didn't see how a quick look-see at an import-export company in the middle of the day could be forbiddingly dangerous. I could always come back for any serious business.

I began regretting my decision the moment I rang the buzzer, and my unease increased when I saw the seediness of the area in which the company was located; it wasn't the kind of neighborhood where you'd bother with a showroom. Neptune seemed uncomfortable too; she laughed and joked as always, but her good humor seemed forced, a bubbling exterior masking tension. Once I stopped and suggested she take a cab back, but she wouldn't hear of it. I didn't feel like arguing, and decided I'd get the business out of the way as quickly as possible. Eventually we both fell into silence.

The address I was looking for turned out to be a ramshackle seven-story building crowding the East River. I placed its date of construction at around the time of Columbus; its red brick facade was turning to blood-colored sand before the onslaught of the city's corrosive air. In the rear was a parking lot strewn with litter and separated from the river by a rusted iron fence.

The directory in the lobby indicated that the Iranian Import-Export Company was on the fourth floor. There was a choice between a sick-looking elevator and a dimly lighted stairway that might have been copied from an illustration in a gothic novel. Feeling lucky, I decided we'd take our chances with the elevator.

The building might be falling apart, but business was brisk on the fourth floor; a coffee cart pushed by its consumptive-looking attendant rumbled through the halls. I found the administrative offices at the end of the corridor, knocked once on the frosted glass door and walked in.

A pretty, braless blond looked up and smiled. "May I help you?"

"My name's Frederickson, and this is my assistant, Miss—uh—Hafez."

The secretary raised her eyebrows. "Oh? Like the poet?"

"Right." I knew I'd gotten the name from somewhere.

"May I ask the nature of your business?"

"Oh, I don't know. We might be interested in a large consignment of Persian rugs."

"And *ghandeils*," Neptune added. "If they're the right price, of course."

The woman picked up the telephone on her desk and pushed a red button. "Mr. Bannon? A Mr. Frederickson and Miss Hafez here to see you."

"Time for you to leave," I said, turning quickly to Neptune. I took a ten-dollar bill from my wallet and held it out to her. "I've decided I want to handle this deal by myself."

Neptune understandably looked bewildered. "But I don't—"

"Take a cab. I'll call you later."

"Mongo," she said imploringly, hurt in her eyes, "what's the matter?"

"Get out!" I said sharply, shoving the bill into her palm and closing her fingers around it. "I'll explain when I call you!"

To my great relief, Neptune—stunned but compliant—turned and went out the door. The embarrassed secretary ushered me into the inner sanctum.

Orrin Bannon looked as surprised to see me as I was to see him. I recovered first; the hand he shoved toward me was wet, and the smile on his face might have been lifted from a cheap makeup kit. "Fancy meeting you here," I said easily.

"Frederickson," Bannon said tightly. "It's nice to see you again. I forgot to tell you how much Soussan and I enjoyed your company the other evening."

"You fooled me completely."

"Soussan scolded me severely when we got home."

I went to the window and looked down; the parking lot was below me, slightly blurred by the smoke-colored air. A rutted dirt road led from the lot to a dump directly beside the dark, sluggish waters of the river.

"I was told there were two of you," Bannon said softly.

"My assistant had to go home."

"I didn't know you were a Persian-carpet fancier, Mr. Frederickson."

"Did John Simpson like Persian rugs?" I turned in time to watch the changes take place on Bannon's face; he ended wearing the expression of a man who's just been kicked in the groin. I tried to keep it that way. "He was here, wasn't he? John Simpson was right here in this room!"

Bannon swallowed hard. "I don't know what you're talking about. Who's this John Simpson?"

Aside from a tic that had suddenly appeared in the right corner of his mouth, Bannon seemed to be regaining his composure. I went after him again. "You know goddamn well who John Simpson is—or was. He's the man who got himself killed trying to track down a young man who's been calling himself Mehdi Zahedi." I paused for effect. "Zahedi's real name is probably Nasser Razvan," I continued, invoking the name Simpson had circled on the Iran Air passenger list.

Bannon blanched, and his Adam's apple bobbed up and down like a broken yo-yo. "You must be crazy," he said unconvincingly. "We meet once and here you are in my office talking nonsense. If I remember right, you were looking for some missing circus performer."

"Hassan Khordad. Was he one of your imports?"

"I don't know what you're talking about." His nose and the area around his sideburns had turned a flame-colored red.

"You know Hassan Khordad. You may even have gone to The Santur with him once or twice. You were afraid the dancer would remember, so you slipped her a hundred dollars not to talk to me. You should have been more generous; two hundred more loosened her right up."

"Who're you working for, Frederickson?"

"The Hassan Khordad fan club."

"Well, freak, I say you're a smart-ass. And I don't see what any of this has to do with me."

"You're somehow tied in with Hassan Khordad and Mehdi Zahedi. That means you probably had something to do with the murder of John Simpson." I pointed out the window toward the water. "There's the river where Simpson was found; right on your doorstep. A very convenient place to dispose of an unwanted body. Why Simpson, Bannon? What was it he found out? And where the hell is Hassan Khordad?"

Bannon was trying to appear calm, but the panicky glitter in his eyes betrayed him. His knuckles were white where they gripped the edge of his desk. "An import-export company would make a convenient cover for an espionage ring," I continued. "It would be easy as hell to shuttle information back and forth with whatever legitimate goodies you handle. Somehow, Simpson found that out when he connected you with Mehdi Zahedi; maybe you'd been keeping an eye on Zahedi for your friend Khordad. Whatever Simpson found out was enough to get him killed. I don't know who's protecting you, and I can't prove anything yet, but you'd better believe I'm sure as hell going to try. I'll begin by writing a few letters to Senators and Congressmen. I think we may already have enough to warrant a Congressional investigation. What do *you* think?"

"That's enough, Frederickson."

My initial reaction to the sight of the gun in his hand was elation that I'd apparently struck a moving target dead center. Then the fear came. "Don't be more of an idiot than you already are, Bannon. You shoot off that forty-four and you'll deafen the whole floor. You'll have one hell of a time explaining why there's a dead dwarf bleeding all over your expensive carpet."

"The room's soundproofed," Bannon said with a touch of pride. "No one will hear." He picked up the phone on his desk and pushed a button. He mumbled something in Farsi, just slowly enough for me to catch my name.

"It still means you'll have another body to dispose of," I said, staring into the single eye of the gun. Loaded guns pointed in my direction make me say silly things: they hadn't had any trouble getting rid of Simpson, and I was considerably smaller. I started to maneuver for position. The gun followed; I stood still. "If you're going to kill me, the least you can do is tell me what this is all about. What happened to Khordad and Zahedi?"

Bannon said nothing as he sat back down in his chair and leaned on the desk. The gun didn't waver, and that was enough to convince me he knew how to use it. I might have tried a quick roll up against the desk, but that could have brought things to a head: my head. I didn't want to rush things. For the moment, Bannon didn't seem in any hurry to kill me.

"Were you recruited from the beginning, or did you just kind of fall into this line of work?"

"This country could learn a lot from Iran," he said, nervously tugging at a sideburn. "There's order there; niggers don't riot and kikes don't run things."

"God save us from the screwball amateurs," I said.

Bannon flushed and rose from his chair. He looked as if he wanted to come around from behind the desk and hit me with the gun. I'd have liked that; I was sure I could take him at close range. But the problem became academic when the door opened and two Iranians entered the office.

One was tall and frail-looking; the ravages of smallpox had left his face looking like a map of the moon. His partner, on the other hand, had somehow found room for what I estimated to be upwards of two hundred and fifty pounds on a five-foot-six frame. His face was puffy and jaundiced, lined with broken veins. He was constantly belching and breaking wind; I doubted he was invited to many social functions. They were a decidedly unmatched pair.

I was surprised to see that their presence had done nothing to tranquilize Bannon; if anything, Bannon's face was even paler, and his hands had begun to tremble. I wondered what he was afraid of.

I laid on one of the Persian insults Darius had taught me. My pronunciation must have left something to be desired; the fat man farted, while his partner began to circle to my left. I shifted my feet, knowing that if they both got close enough to me at the same time, I might be able to make a move. What they didn't know about this dwarf could kill them.

Fatty said something to Bannon in Farsi and took the gun. I planted my right foot, ready to pivot, but it was too late. The other man had already stepped behind me and had one of his bony forearms across my windpipe. The edges of my vision immediately began to blur. I drove my elbow back, aiming for his groin, and missed. By this time he had a chloroformed rag over my nose and mouth. He eased the pressure on my windpipe and I involuntarily sucked in the sickly-sweet fumes. I rode a long, screaming siren down into a spongy pit that smelled like a hospital.

8

"WAKE UP, dwarf."

Hassan Khordad's voice was soft, almost gentle, with a thick regional accent. However, his face was even uglier than his publicity photos indicated, and I told him so. He smiled without mirth and stepped closer to me. His right arm dangled lifelessly at his side, as though it were on vacation from the rest of his body.

"I'm not going to waste words, dwarf," Khordad said in the same soft tone. "Who sent you after me?"

"Local One-Twelve of the Weight Lifters' Union. It seems you haven't paid your dues."

His left hand flicked out and caught me across the mouth; it had been a casual, easy swing, but it rattled my teeth and made my ears ring. For a moment I thought I'd lose consciousness. A few blows like that in the right places could kill a man; I'd have to try to watch my mouth.

I was bound to a chair, my arms stretched painfully around the back of the chair and my ankles lashed to the legs. I feigned dizziness while I tested the ropes. Whoever had tied me had done a fairly competent job, but I was confident that with a little muscle control, I could get out. If I had the time. The trouble was that Hassan Khordad acted like a man in a hurry, and he had company. The two Iranians who'd done a number on me in Bannon's office were standing against the wall to my left. The emaciated one had his arms crossed, while his obese partner continued to belch, covering his mouth alternately with one hand, then the other. Still, even with one arm dangling useless at his side, Hassan Khordad was obviously the man in charge.

The furnishings and paintings on the walls of the room I was in spelled money. The door to the room was closed, so I couldn't see into the rest of the house, but I judged from the oaken beams in the ceiling that it was old.

Khordad snapped his fingers and the man with the scarred face went to a dresser in the corner, opened a drawer and produced a large yellow oilcloth. It appeared that Khordad had certain sensibilities; he didn't want to get blood on the carpets. But I was wrong. The thin man took the cloth into another room, then returned, grabbed himself between the legs and whispered something into the fat man's ear. Both men laughed; they were making me very nervous.

"Simpson shot you, didn't he?" I asked, gesturing with my head toward Khordad's dangling arm. "He must have severed a few nerves. That's why you couldn't go back to the circus." Khordad was staring at me intently, seemingly as curious about me as I was about him. "How am I doing so far?"

Khordad half-smiled, but his raisin eyes seemed too bright. "Very good," he said. "I think I'm going to give you a prize."

"Simpson was trailing Mehdi Zahedi and he stumbled across Bannon's operation," I wheezed. "Bannon pushed the panic button and you came running. You ambushed Simpson in Bannon's office, but it wasn't as easy as you'd thought it was going to be. You managed to break Simpson's back, but not before he'd put a few bullets into your arm. Bannon found himself with one dead detective and a crippled assassin. You couldn't very well go to a hospital, but you probably have people ready for just such emergencies. They wheeled you away, but Bannon had to dispose of Simpson himself. He took him down in the freight elevator to his car, then dumped him in the river. But there was a hitch. Bannon was in such a snit that he forgot to empty Simpson's pockets. How's that?"

"I've listened patiently to you, dwarf," Khordad said in his curious, slow manner. "I'll continue to listen patiently while you tell me who sent you after me, and why."

"Did you kill the kid who was calling himself Mehdi Zahedi?" Khordad stopped in the middle of a swing and looked at me strangely. For the first time his eyes reflected uncertainty. I swallowed blood and kept talking. "Why are you sticking around? You're well enough to travel."

He hesitated a moment, then reached into his pocket. The huge hand came out holding the notebook I'd taken from his trunk. He spoke very softly. "Why did you take these things, dwarf? Who's paying you?"

"I can't remember," I said, certain that whatever Khordad didn't know was all that was keeping me alive.

"Then I will give you your prize."

Khordad surprised me by snapping his fingers again instead of hitting me. The thin man disappeared once more into the other room. When he returned, my stomach contracted involuntarily, forcing the breath out of me in a single, explosive rush; my heartbeat fluttered, then began to pound inside my chest. The "prize" Khordad had mentioned was Neptune. Her mouth was taped, and her hands were bound tightly behind her back. The thin man tore the adhesive tape from her mouth with one quick motion.

"Mongo!" Neptune cried, her eyes wide with terror. "Don't tell them anything you don't—"

The thin man pulled on her hair, snapping her head back. A stiletto had suddenly appeared in his hand, and he ran its edge softly up and down the line of her throat.

"For God's sake, Khordad," I said, struggling to keep my voice even. "Let's be reasonable. Now, you're going to let the woman go . . . and I'm going to *watch* her go. Then you and I are going to sit down calmly and have a long chat. I don't know very much to begin with, but you can have every bit of it. Okay?"

Khordad smiled and nodded his head. I began to relax. Then the strongman gave an almost imperceptible nod of his head; the two men suddenly grabbed Neptune by the arms and dragged her into the other room. The door slammed shut. I arched my back and struggled desperately against the ropes, but managed only to tip over the chair and bang my head painfully on the floor. Khordad effortlessly picked up the chair with his good hand and righted it.

Then Neptune began to scream. The horrible, banshee wailing carried easily through the closed door.

"Now will you answer my questions, dwarf?"

"Wh . . . what?" Khordad had spoken so softly that I could barely hear him. Also, the sound of Neptune's torment was disorienting me, making me numb, threatening to hurl me into some kind of silent, alternative universe where a certain stupid dwarf private detective would have a second chance to undo a stupid mistake.

"I want to know all about what you've been up to in this matter. From the beginning."

"Yes," I heard myself saying. My voice was distant, hollow, like a drugged man's. "Of course. What's the matter with you? But I can't think; make them stop so I can *think!*"

"No," Khordad said easily. "They will stop torturing your

friend when I tell them to, and I will give that order only when I have satisfactory answers to all my questions."

I imagined I heard something click inside me—a sensation of ears popping at high altitude. Then I heard myself start to talk. While I cringed inside myself against the agony of Neptune's pain, my voice quickly and efficiently spun out the answers to Khordad's questions. After what seemed an eternity but was probably no more than four or five minutes, Khordad shouted and the screaming abruptly stopped. The silence that suddenly fell in the house was almost as bad. There was not a sound from the other room. The two men reappeared, closed the door quietly behind them, leaned back against the wall and exchanged smiles. I sighed and closed my eyes.

"So *Statler* sent you after me." Khordad sounded surprised. "Why would Statler spend his money to hire a private detective to find me?"

"What have you done with the woman?"

"The woman will be taken care of. Answer me."

"I *did*!"

"I want to hear it again." He started to turn toward the thin man.

"Statler's a funny guy," I said quickly. "It was a matter of pride. You were important to him, and your absence was costing him money. He wanted to find out what had happened to you; he was going to either try to help you or sue you for breach of contract."

"That's stupid; it's just throwing good money after bad."

My mouth tasted of bile. I swallowed, trying to work up some moisture on my tongue. I got blood instead. "He gave you a break and you took off on him. He just wanted to settle accounts."

Khordad chuckled, and the muscles in his good arm rippled. "I believe you, dwarf. It's very funny." He glanced at his watch, then turned to the two men. "Kill him as we discussed," he said. "I have business. I'll call in an hour to make sure the job has been done properly."

The English had been for my benefit—one more turn of the screw. I suddenly knew without doubt that they intended to kill both Neptune and me, and there was nothing I could do about it. My reaction was rage. I leaned forward and spat into Khordad's face. Calmly, without a trace of anger in his face, he stepped forward and hit me once, expertly, in the side with the edge of his good hand. I felt ribs crack. I slumped forward, struggling to remain conscious. Khordad repeated his instructions in Farsi to make sure the men understood, then turned and walked out the door.

The door closed behind Khordad and the two men came toward me. The thought of dying like a trussed turkey enraged me. I leaned farther forward against the ropes and felt a stab of pain in my side. The fat man drew a gun and pointed it at my head. I tensed, wondering how many milliseconds of life were left, waiting for the bullet to smash into my future. But the bullet didn't come; the fat man kept his gun trained on me while his skinny partner cut my bonds with his knife. I went limp again and closed my eyes, trying to think.

I could see they didn't want me found with a bullet in me, which meant they had something else in mind. The fat man grabbed my shirt and lifted me to my feet. Khordad's hammer hand had drained the strength from my arms and legs. The searing pain that racked my side was all that I had to hold on to, all that was keeping me conscious.

The fat man let go of me and I sagged to my knees, then flopped over onto my good side and twitched my legs. I thought it was a great performance, and I could only hope that the two men were buying tickets.

The fat one cursed and shook his gun at me. I moaned.

The other one stepped forward and jammed the toe of his shoe into my side, just inches away from my broken ribs. I groaned and rolled my eyes. The men exchanged a few words, then put their weapons away. They teamed up to lift me by my arms and ankles; then we were off through the door. We passed under a chandelier, through a room filled with draped furniture, and then outside onto a bright expanse of manicured green. That surprised me. I'd assumed we were still inside the factory building.

The sun was warm on my upturned face. I squinted against the sunlight and could see that we were heading around the side of the house toward a grove of trees. I made a mental inventory of how much of me was left in working order; everything hurt, but I was fairly certain I could make the pieces move when I had to. Sounds and shapes around me had an annoying habit of sliding into and out of focus, and I wondered if I were bleeding internally. My arms were growing numb where the thin man held me in his strong, bony fingers.

What annoyed me almost as much as the fact that the two men intended to kill me was that I hadn't even begun to unravel the whole story of Khordad's contact at the university, a missing student leader who wasn't who he said he was, American superguns and ruined cities.

We came out of the trees, threading along a narrow path on the edge of the sheer escarpment that was the New Jersey Palisades. To the south, the George Washington Bridge gleamed in the sunlight; below, at the base of the cliff, the dark, oily Hudson rolled along its littered banks. Across the river, New York lay sedentary under a steely-blue haze of smoky air.

The two men stepped off the path and carried me toward the edge of the cliff. It was a perfectly logical move; a fall to the rocks below would be just as permanent as a bullet, and there'd be no lead for the police to dig out of me. They stopped at the edge, looked at each other, then started to swing me. It was time to see which parts of me would still do what I wanted them to do.

I waited until the last possible moment, at the top of a swing. Up until that moment I'd remained completely limp, and as a result the men were completely off guard, paying no more attention to me than they might to a bag of sand. Now I arched my back, going for additional height. Thousands of knife-edged steel bands twisted back and forth around my broken ribs; but pain was life, and I embraced it, using it as a mental springboard to launch myself at the men who would kill me. At the top of my arch I pulled my right leg back sharply, freeing it from the fat man's loose grip. I brought the leg back to my chest, then snapped it forward, slashing the razor in the tip of my shoe across his throat. He screamed, and the scream became a gurgle. He let go of my other leg and sat down hard on the grass.

The thin man still had hold of my arms. I twisted hard, breaking his grip. I felt something snap in my left side and I knew that a rib had broken clean; but the side was growing numb, and I had other things to worry about besides the pain. I hit the ground on my shoulder and rolled to my feet, praying that the jagged end of the rib would stay clear of my lung.

The pain returned, rolling through me like some great tidal wave from hell. Everything was tinted red, and in the middle of that scarlet sea the thin man was reaching for his knife. I lurched forward and flicked the tip of my shoe across his shinbone. He yelped and jackknifed forward. I drove a stiff thumb up into his face; it hit his cheekbone, then skidded to the side and buried itself in something soft.

The man's screams climbed the scale. I watched as he reeled backward, chanting his pain in a high-pitched, wavering squeal. He took one step too many, teetered for a moment on the cliff edge, then disappeared over the lip of the escarpment.

I staggered around in a circle, groping blindly. My vision cleared in time for me to see the fat man, still in a sitting position, shudder, then stiffen as the last of the life in him drained out. I wobbled to the edge of the escarpment and retched. Far below, the thin man's broken body lay sprawled among the rocks.

Gradually my head cleared and I started to sort out the excruciating pains from those that were merely torturous. So far, the broken end of the rib had stayed clear of my vital organs, but I couldn't be sure how long my good fortune would last; the slightest move in the wrong direction and I'd undoubtedly end up with a punctured lung.

Moving very slowly and carefully, I walked over to the fat man's body, took his gun and walked just as carefully back to the house. I managed to get inside, then—keeping my back very straight—gingerly eased myself down on the floor, bracing myself against a desk on which there was a telephone. I pulled the phone to the floor by yanking on the cord, picked up the receiver and started to dial Garth's precinct. Then I slowly replaced the receiver in its cradle.

First and foremost, I had to find out what Khordad had done with Neptune; if I called the police in now, I might never know. My only hope lay in the possibility that Khordad would return. If he did, I'd know what to do with him.

And there was another reason I didn't yet want to call the police. A jagged memory had surged up from a dark place: Kaznakov, the Russian. Stronger than the pain, welling up from a deep font in my soul, was a poisonous geyser of rage. After I found out what he'd done with Neptune, I wanted Khordad to feel some of the pain he'd so casually administered to the two of us. Khordad, with the same last initial and mildly abrasive personality, strongly reminded me of the Russian.

For a long time after the session with Kaznakov I'd been out of my mind, not only from lingering pain but from the *memory* of the pain and, most of all, terror that the Russian would find out I was still alive and come back to finish the job he'd started. By the grace of Victor Rafferty's strange talents, I'd been able to overcome my terror and kill Kaznakov. But Rafferty wasn't around to bail me out this time, and I wasn't about to go through that same mental torture again, to wake screaming in the middle of the night, certain that Khordad, with his soft voice and deadly hands, was waiting for me outside my bedroom door. This particular exorcism would have to be a solo performance. I knew I would hear Neptune's screams for the rest of my life, and there was nothing I could do about that; that was the totally inadequate price I'd have to pay for my stupidity. But I wanted Khordad to pay with the only thing I could extract —*his* life.

The ringing of the telephone jarred me. That would be Khordad checking on his lieutenants. I counted the rings: twenty. The ringing stopped for a few seconds, then started again; fifteen rings this time, then silence. I gripped the dead man's gun in my hand and settled down to wait. I could only hope that Khordad would return alone.

He did. Night had fallen, and I'd left a light on in an outer room while I sat by the desk in the dark. I saw the Iranian come through the front door, gun in hand. He glanced around, then moved toward the open door of the room where I was waiting. He was silhouetted plainly as he reached inside for the wall switch. When the lights came on, he saw me and grunted with surprise. I shot him in the left arm, aiming high for the collarbone. He yelled with pain and rage, then spun, clawing at the wall.

"What did you do with the woman, you big fuck?" I couldn't recognize my own voice.

Khordad had slipped to one knee. He slowly pulled himself to his feet and braced himself against the wall. Disembodied words were banging around inside my head; I had to pick out the ones I wanted and force them from my throat. It was only then that I realized I was crying. For Neptune; for Garth. For myself. "Where's the woman!" I screamed, sobbing. "Did you kill her?"

Khordad pushed himself off the wall and staggered toward me, both arms now dangling useless at his sides. Steadying the gun with both hands, I shot him in the right leg. This time he made no sound as he went down. The only sign of his agony was the flesh of his face, which had gone chalk white.

"Answer me, goddamn it!" My voice quavered with pain, grief and exhaustion. I knew I was very close to the edge, and so did Khordad.

Incredibly, the Iranian smiled; on his face it was a tortured, obscene expression, a sick grimace that did nothing to hide the rage and terrible pain in his eyes. Defying all the laws of nature, logic and the body's mechanics, Khordad struggled to his feet and came toward me, locking his right leg and shuffling forward, using the momentum of his weight to carry him toward me. His head was lowered like a battering ram. By now my strength was almost gone and I was shaking. If Khordad reached me, I was dead. My vision was blurring and the room had begun to tilt.

I picked Khordad's shape out from the shadows and fired again. The bullet entered through his right cheekbone and he dropped at my feet. I didn't have to move to know he was dead. I managed to dial the operator and give an approximation of where I was before I passed out.

9

WANTING TO GET absolutely everything connected with the case out of the way at the earliest possible moment, I forced myself to call Phil Statler in the morning from the hospital. I told him what had happened. He wanted to talk, but I gently cut him off and hung up. Then Garth came. During the night I'd babbled out the entire story of what had happened, so he never mentioned it. He stared at my chest and asked how I felt. I said I was all right. He nodded, said he'd spoken to the doctor who'd wired me up and that I'd be out of the hospital in a day or two. Then he walked to the window.

The house in New Jersey had belonged to Bannon, whose body had been found in the river. It seemed he'd attracted one too many investigators and Khordad had decided it was time to cut off that particular liability after he'd interrogated me. As far as the authorities from the State Department on down were concerned, I'd become entangled in a foreign espionage operation, and there'd be no publicity at all. No charges would be filed against me, since I'd obviously killed in self-defense; I wouldn't even have to file a deposition. It seemed everyone was overflowing with gratitude, and only the hypersensitivity of the matter prevented the Secretary of State from writing me a personal message. Soussan Bannon had known nothing of her husband's activities, as far as the authorities were concerned, and she was on her way back to Iran. The university was considering making me a full professor. No trace had been found of Neptune, and it was assumed her body had been thoroughly and professionally disposed of by Khordad. For reasons that had died with him, he hadn't wanted her death connected with either Bannon's or mine.

Garth imparted all of this information to me in a flat, robotlike, totally matter-of-fact tone of voice, all the time staring out the window.

"They haven't found her body," I whispered. "Maybe she's still alive." I hated myself the moment I said it. I didn't believe she was alive, and Garth didn't believe she was alive. Neptune had been nothing more than an innocent bystander who'd ended up a witness. After her usefulness to him was over, Khordad had to have blown her out like a candle.

Garth mumbled something I couldn't quite hear. I didn't have to understand the words to know it was a curse. Directed at me.

"Garth," I said, "please turn around and look at me." When he did, I could see that his face was glistening with tears that continued to roll in steady, tiny streams from his bloodshot eyes. "God, brother," I said, tears filling my own eyes, "we have to talk. Do you want me to try to *tell* you how sorry I am?"

"I don't want you to tell me anything," he said. His voice remained perfectly even and flat, which made it all the more eerie. It was as if all his terrible grief were contained in the rivulets of tears that continued to pour from his eyes, drop from his chin to the floor. He made no move to wipe them away.

"Garth," I said, shaking my head back and forth as though that would relieve the pain in my heart. "Oh, brother . . ."

"I said I didn't want you to say anything." Garth closed his eyes, tilted his head back and smiled at some memory. I felt sick. "I've never loved a woman the way I loved Neptune," he continued softly. "It was as . . . if my life had never really come together before she came into it. I was . . . lonely. So lonely."

"Garth," I murmured, not having anything to say but compelled to say something. "I know; I know something about loneliness myself."

Slowly Garth's eyes opened, his head tilted down and his smile collapsed. For the first time he looked directly at me. I wished he hadn't; it wasn't my brother in the room with me. A large part of Garth had died with Neptune. "No, you don't," he said in the same haunted, soft voice. "You know nothing about loneliness; not really. You're a freak, a *famous* freak, and you love it. *Women* love it. You probably fuck more women in a month than I do in a year. You wear what other people assume must be loneliness like a kind of armor. You lonely? I know better. You're too goddamned wrapped up in yourself, in playing Superdwarf, to have a lonely moment.

"Well, you've always been damned fucking lucky. You were lucky *this* time, but Neptune wasn't. Her luck ran out pretty damned fast, didn't it? She got permanently pounded on." He started toward the door, then broke down and sobbed. I could have risen and gone to him, but I could think of no words or gestures that would bridge the terrible wall that had sprung up between us. Finally he pulled himself together, turned, and in a cracked voice said, "By the way, Mongo: I . . . I don't think I ever want to see or talk to you again."

Ali Azad came through the door and almost collided with Garth, who now covered his face with his hands and hurried out. Ali didn't even seem to notice. He asked me how I was; I said I was all right, but I don't think he heard. He wore an appropriate expression of sympathy, but his eyes were out of focus, almost glazed. It occurred to me that I could be hanging off the ceiling by suction cups on my toes and Ali wouldn't notice. He was a young man with something on his distinctly one-track mind. That was fine with me. Garth had deposited a large, growing stone in my stomach; the stone was cold, and I was freezing. I felt tough, mean. I needed someone to play "normal" with; someone, perhaps, to make uncomfortable. Ali filled the bill perfectly: I thought I might have a few shocks for him.

"I heard at the university that you were in the hospital. I am sorry."

"Thanks," I said evenly. "I won't be here long." I pulled the blanket on my bed up to my chin; it did nothing to warm me.

"You found Hassan Khordad?"

"He found me."

Ali studied my swollen face. "He did this to you?"

"He looks worse."

"Where is he?"

"Dead. I killed him."

Azad shook his head. "That is hard to believe, Dr. Frederickson. No offense."

"I'm just one big bundle of surprises," I said without smiling. I watched him as he put his hands in his pockets and stared at the floor. "What's your problem, Ali?"

"I came to see if you were all right."

"And?"

His head came up fast. "I would like to know if you have discovered anything about Mehdi."

"Ali, I think your boy's in Iran."

Ali shook his head again; this time his shoulders moved

with it, and he looked like a rodeo horse trying to buck an unwanted rider. "I have told you that is impossible."

"Sorry, Ali. It's not only possible, it's probable. In fact, as far as Immigration is concerned, there *is* no such person as Mehdi Zahedi."

Azad stumbled backward into a chair and sat down hard. He glanced nervously around the room, then dropped his head and studied the backs of his hands. "I don't understand," he said in a hoarse whisper.

"That makes two of us. All I've got is scraps of information, and the only people I know of who could fit them together are dead or missing." I hesitated, wondering whether it was worth the trouble of going into, decided it was. Talking helped keep the cold away. "Somebody's been running American guns into Iran. Not just any guns; LS-180s, which have a laser-beam component; the last word in Instant Death. Now, hang on to that fact, because it's important. LS-180s aren't the easiest things in the world to get your hands on: every one that leaves the factory is *supposed* to be registered. You sure as hell couldn't mount a gunrunning operation with LS-180s from Iran. The GEM leaders—"

Azad's eyes flashed. "Then you *do* believe—"

"The *GEM* leaders," I continued impatiently, "are in the United States. It makes sense anyway; you don't have your generals wandering around in the middle of the battlefield. Specifically, *the* top man, or at least the logistics chiefs, must have been traced here to New York City by the SAVAK. That's why the SAVAK has been swarming. My guess is that GEM came very close to killing the Shah at last year's Shiraz art festival; I've seen a photograph with a section of scaffolding circled, and the section would be a perfect place to plant *plastique* if you wanted to bring the whole thing tumbling down. The assassination didn't come off and somebody from GEM got caught, but it must have scared the shit out of the

Shah and he started to get *really* serious about finding the leaders."

Ali clapped his hands together; they made a sharp sound that did nothing for my nerves. "Mehdi!" he yelped with delight. "Mehdi is a member of GEM!"

"Uh, not quite. The way I see it, the president of your organization is SAVAK."

"That's not funny, Dr. Frederickson," Ali said icily. "We are serious men."

"Ali, I'll lay odds that your glorious leader's real name is Nasser Razvan." I watched the young Iranian's dark eyes cloud with anger. "Sorry, Ali, but that's the way it stacks up. Nasser Razvan flew to Iran by first-class jet the same night Mehdi Zahedi disappeared. I don't know why; maybe something came up that required his personal attention. Somehow, Simpson found out that Razvan and your president were one and the same, and he had to be killed. When I stumbled on the same trail, *I* had to be killed."

Ali's face was mottled with dark, purplish patches. "It *can't* be true. The things he spoke of—"

"Talk's cheap, Ali."

"I tell you it is *impossible!*" Trembling, he rose to his feet. "If Mehdi is such a clever spy, why didn't he return here immediately? Why would the SAVAK keep him in Iran so long that suspicions would be raised?"

"I haven't got the slightest idea."

"Of course you don't! You don't know because you are guessing!"

"Hey, pal, I *said* I was guessing. *You* guess for a while if you want to. Put all the facts into your head, shake them around a bit and see if they don't spell SAVAK. Start off with the fact that Immigration's never heard of any Mehdi Zahedi."

"It is a mistake!" Ali's voice, thick with confusion, was a

plea. "You know those bureaucrats! They are *always* making these stupid mistakes!"

"All right, Ali, you believe what you want to; I really don't give a shit. I told you I'd let you know if I thought I had a line on your man, and that's what I've done."

There was a long silence. When Ali spoke again, his words were high-pitched and run together. "Dr. Frederickson, would you be willing to go to Iran?"

I laughed, then choked as pain ripped through my side. "You've got to be kidding," I whispered. "If I'm right about Zahedi, and after all that's happened, can you imagine the reception the SAVAK would have prepared for me? Do I look as if I had a death wish?"

Ali frowned. "You are an American citizen; I do not think the Iranian Government would dare to harm you. If they do know about your part in killing Khordad, it is more likely they will simply refuse to let you into the country; it is only Iranians that they care to torture and kill. We would pay you very well for making the effort."

"I don't speak the language."

"That can be taken care of. There is no one else we can trust, and you know the background of the case. We would arrange for somebody to meet you in Tehran. In the meantime, we will arrange for cassette tapes and a language tutor."

"What would I be expected to do?"

"We would simply like you to make discreet inquiries through your interpreter. We would like you to try to determine if Mehdi is in Iran and, if so, what has happened to him. We will pay all your expenses, plus ten thousand dollars."

I repeated the figure just to make sure I'd heard right, and he nodded. "All that just to find out what happened to Mehdi Zahedi?"

"Yes. He is very important to us."

"That's a *lot* of money, Ali."

"Donated expressly for the purpose of solving the mystery of what has happened to Mehdi." He cleared his throat. "The money came with the stipulation that we hire you."

"Oh-oh. So much for my anonymity. Who came up with the money?"

The Iranian flushed. "I don't know. But that isn't unusual. I have already told you that much of our money comes from Iranians who, for their own reasons, want to remain anonymous."

"Ali, it's time you started thinking with your head instead of your guts. That money's a gilt-edged invitation to me from the SAVAK."

"Why should the SAVAK spend so much money to bring you to Iran? It would be much cheaper to kill you here."

"When did you get this money?"

"Yesterday, by messenger."

"It doesn't matter where the money came from. How does a foreigner—a dwarf, no less—go about making 'discreet' inquiries through an interpreter? The idea is absurd. You'll really screw them if you just put the money in the bank. Better yet, print up some leaflets."

"But it is *our* money, and we want to hire you to find Mehdi. If you believe Mehdi is in Iran, then it is there you must go. We will prepare a dossier containing absolutely everything we know about him."

"I've already seen the information you gave John Simpson. It read like a press release. How much can you add to that?"

He dropped his eyes. "Admittedly, not much. But will you at least think about going, Dr. Frederickson?"

"I *did* think about it," I said, raising my eyebrows. "I thought about it for half a second when you first brought it up, and I gave you my answer."

128

Ali looked confused. "But . . . I don't understand. I thought by . . . your questions . . ."

The pain that ran up through my side when I leaned forward was almost welcome; it gave me something to focus on besides the terrible, spiked rock in my gut. "I ask questions because I'm naturally curious. As far as I'm concerned, I'll be quite content if I live the rest of my life without hearing of Iran, or meeting another Iranian. That includes you, kid. Have a nice day. Goodbye."

I filled most of my days with classes, research, books, movies, concerts—anything that would tone down the volume of Neptune's screams inside my head. I still heard them when I slept. Still, I managed to function; there was nothing else to do.

I gave Garth three weeks. Then, after classes, I went over to his precinct station house. Harry Stans looked up from his *Daily News* as I walked in. "Hey, Mongo! How you feeling?"

"Okay, Harry. Thanks. How about yourself?"

"Terrific. I was just getting ready to call you. Where the hell is Garth?"

"What are you talking about?" I said tightly.

"When's he coming back from Iran?"

A nervous tic I'd developed in my right eyelid suddenly began fluttering. I pressed the heel of my hand hard against it. "I didn't know he was in Iran."

"He didn't *tell* you?"

"Why did he go, Harry? Do you know?"

Harry, puzzled, looked at me strangely for a few moments, then shrugged. "Well, you must know he was off the wall for days after Neptune's death. Then he got a message from the girl's family inviting him to come there and visit them for her funeral. He took a week's vacation time, but he was supposed to be back a week and a half ago. Well, not a word from him, and there's been some heavy breathing from the brass. But we've been holding them off; we know how screwed up he's been since Neptune's death."

"What part of Iran does her family live in?"

"Don't know, pal. I never saw the message; Garth just mentioned it to me. Anyway, if he gets in touch with you, tell him to get it together and get his ass in here." Harry paused, scratched his head. "Shit, if he'd just waited a couple of days he'd have had something nice to take back to her family."

"What's that, Harry?"

"Her jewelry box. It ain't worth much, but Neptune was worried because it's a family heirloom. Anyway, whoever burglarized her apartment made a mistake: they pawned the box. It's amazing what some of these jerks will do for a couple of extra bucks. *Now* we think we've got a lead on who's fencing her jewelry."

"Terrific," I said.

No one at the Celanese Corporation would give me any information about Neptune's background or family. I went back to my apartment and wrote a long report on everything I knew and suspected about the case, a list of media people who were to follow up on it, and a covering letter taped to the outside with instructions to open the report if I wasn't heard from in four weeks. That would go to Phil Statler. I updated my will, then called Ali.

II

IRAN

10

FOR A WEEK I worked my tutor overtime during the day, and spent most of my nights immersed in the language tapes Ali had provided me with, along with three volumes of Farsi–English dictionaries. I didn't get much sleep, but if I was right about Garth's absence being a second, command invitation, I'd have plenty of time to catch up on my sleep—perhaps forever. At least I'd be able to chat with my captors in pidgin Farsi. I didn't see that I had any choice but to go, and the SAVAK knew it. One person had already died for my sins, and it was time to pay my dues. I stayed with the tapes all through the flight, then dropped them and my recorder into a toilet wastebasket.

Seen from the air, Tehran seemed no more than a dusty, blurred adjunct of the desert; in fact, it was the latest Shangri-La for every hustling high roller in the world, the end of the rainbow floating on a subterranean sea of black, bubbling gold. It was as if, on this section of the planet, Nature had painted only from the earth end of the palette, and the people, living as they did in the midst of brown sand, rock and mountains, knew no other colors and could build only in terms of their immediate surroundings. Or perhaps it was the desert which altered everything to suit its own taste. All of the buildings were the color of the surrounding earth. The rest was desert and barren, rolling mountains. The plane banked. Somewhere in the distance, to the east, was a flash of blue that could have been water.

My cholera shots hurt, and I knew I was running a slight fever. The woman at the consulate where I'd picked up my visa had insisted there was no cholera in Iran, but I'd remembered Darius' words on the subject and taken the series of shots anyway. The doctor's remark that the vaccine, under the best of conditions, was only about forty percent effective would be a sobering reminder to carefully watch what I ate and drank, assuming I had a choice of cuisine. There was no doubt in my mind that even the runt of any cholera litter would cackle with joy at the sight of my soft, relatively sterile Western innards.

The 747 came in to a smooth landing, and I watched out the window as the plane rolled over the broad gray strips of concrete laid out across the sand. Once the plane abruptly braked to a halt as a khaki-colored military jet swooped low over us and landed on the runway a few hundred yards ahead. There were large pieces of artillery and soldiers in jeeps with machine guns lining all the runways, reminders of the tensions in the Middle East and the pervading paranoia that is the ugly court jester in most dictatorial regimes.

Most of my fellow passengers were Iranians, who stared openly at me. In that respect these people, with their dusky, rugged beauty, were no different from the people of Los Angeles, or New York, or Chicago; I was a dwarf, and thus an object of curiosity. However, a good rapport had been established when they'd discovered I could carry on the rudiments of a conversation in their language.

The plane finally rolled to a stop beside a gleaming terminal at the end of the runway. Outside the window, armed soldiers, their weapons nestled in the crooks of their folded arms, stared impassively out at the desert. I remained in my seat while the others rose and filed out. Only then, in the name of optimism, did I reach into my pocket and take out the slip of paper on which Ali had written the name of my contact in Iran: one Parviz Maher, who was supposed to be a student at Tehran University and who worked as a professional tourist guide during the summers. I tore the paper into small pieces and dropped them into the ashtray. According to the plan, Maher was supposed to meet me at the airport. It was his job to find me; my job was to stand around looking like a dwarf.

I felt no guilt at taking Ali's money, which I'd promptly put in the bank. I'd made it very clear to him that I considered my chances for success to be nonexistent. My pessimism hadn't seemed to make any difference; for Ali, it was enough that I'd agreed to go.

The Tehran airport, located at the western edge of the city, was not particularly large, despite the fact that it serviced the nation's capital. The dry, hot air of the early morning was exhilarating, and I walked briskly toward the terminal, stopping briefly to gaze at the mountains in the distance.

There was someone waiting for me inside the terminal, but it wasn't Parviz Maher—not unless the student guide had recently been drafted into the officer corps of the Iranian army. Not surprisingly, the officer spotted me immediately and came forward with the braced stride that is the universal stamp of the military man. Responding to instinct, the muscles in my legs bunched under me and I half-turned, prepared to sprint back out onto the runway. I stayed where I was, my rational mind reminding me why I'd come in the first place—to make a simple trade-off. Besides, with eight thousand miles and an ocean separating me from home, there weren't too many places for me to run.

A glance to my right showed that another officer was closing in on me from that direction, and I didn't have to look behind or to my left to know that there were men there too: I could feel them. None of them carried guns; considering the armored division hanging out on the runway, they obviously didn't feel the need.

The first officer, a tall, trim man with sharp, angular features and smoky, hooded eyes, stopped a few paces in front of me and clicked his polished heels together. We stared at each other for a few moments; then the man pressed the palms of his hands together and bent forward at the waist in an elaborate bow.

"Dr. Frederickson," the man said in passable English, "I am Captain Mohammed Zand. Welcome to Iran."

That wasn't exactly what I'd expected to hear, and I blinked. The men behind and to my left had stopped a short distance away. The officer on my right, a young man with soft, delicate features, approached, bowed and grabbed my luggage. His eyes were open and friendly.

"*Salaam*," I ventured wryly.

Both men grinned. They seemed immensely pleased. "*Salaam, salaam*," the young man said. He glanced at his superior, and Zand nodded. The young man put down one of my suitcases and extended his hand. I shook it.

"Unfortunately, the lieutenant cannot speak English," Zand said. "But he too bids you welcome."

"Where's Garth?"

"Excuse me?"

"Come on. I'm here, so you've got no more need for Garth. You win, so let's play fair and let him go."

"I'm sorry, Dr. Frederickson, I understand your words,

but they have no meaning for me. Perhaps you could explain further."

"Never mind." Obviously, it was game time, and I had no choice but to continue playing and hope for an eventual peek at the rule book.

"Would you come with us, please?" Zand asked politely.

"I'd like to call the American Embassy," I said evenly.

"Of course." Zand smiled. "In fact, we'll be going right by there. Perhaps you would care to attend to your business in person."

"Uh, yeah. I'd like that fine."

"After you finish your business at the embassy, I am sure you would like to rest up. You must be tired after your flight. We have taken the liberty of making a reservation in your name at one of our better hotels. Would four o'clock be convenient?"

"Convenient for what?"

"Oh, I am sorry. We would be proud if you would agree to see our city. Four o'clock is a good time because it is cooler then. With your permission, I will serve as your guide during your stay in Tehran."

Zand and his subordinate had a good act. The young lieutenant carried my luggage as Zand led the way toward Customs. The smoky-eyed captain muttered a few words to the customs inspector, who smiled nervously and let us pass through without even a cursory glance at my luggage. I was impressed.

"Mehrabad Airport is not as big as Kennedy Airport," Zand said conversationally. "I know; I have been to your country."

"Mehrabad is cleaner."

We exchanged a few more pleasantries as we passed through the gates of Mehrabad, past the main entrance and over to the curb, where a long black Mercedes-Benz was waiting, its chauffeur standing rigidly at attention on the sidewalk next to the car's open doors. Zand snapped a finger and the chauffeur moved to the rear door and bowed low. I got into the back seat. The lieutenant got into the front beside the chauffeur, while Zand positioned himself beside me. As the car pulled away, Zand leaned forward and spoke a few words to the driver. I caught the words "American Embassy."

"Maybe I'll wait until later to visit the embassy," I heard myself saying. "You're right; I'm tired now." If Zand was so willing to take me to the embassy, I could see it would do me no good to go there. I could imagine the embassy officials' reaction to my story that the two smiling army officers in the chauffeured limousine outside had dropped me off so that I could report my brother's kidnapping.

"As you wish," Zand said. He gave new directions to the driver, and in slightly less than an hour we were outside the plush Tehran Hilton, northwest of the city.

It seemed a good time to ask for a look at the rule book. "The hotel looks very pleasant," I said. "Now why don't you tell me where my brother is?"

Zand shrugged, looking sincerely pained. "I still do not understand why you ask about your brother. I know nothing of this."

"Then tell me what you plan to do with *me*."

He smiled. "You are tired now. We will talk later. In the meantime, if there is anything I can do to help make your stay more comfortable, please call me. The man at the desk will put you in touch with me immediately. Remember, you are our guest. Please do not hesitate to ask for anything."

There didn't seem to be much point in arguing, so I didn't. The bell captain took my suitcases and hurried inside, where he waited, holding the elevator doors open for me.

"Until four o'clock, Dr. Frederickson," Zand said. He waved and disappeared back into the brown leather depths of the Mercedes. The lieutenant was still looking back and smiling as the car pulled away from the curb and merged with the rest of the traffic.

Inside the hotel, the bell captain and two assistants did everything but carry me bodily up to my room. The bell captain took my passport, and I gave the three of them a good tip.

My accommodations had to be the equivalent of the Presidential Suite; there was a large patio overlooking a garden in the middle of a large inner courtyard. In the center of the room, midway between the bath and a huge double bed, was a small, tiled reflecting pool. The sheets of the bed had already been pulled back, and an array of English-language magazines and newspapers was neatly stacked on a mahogany stand beside the bed. I kicked off my shoes, removed my jacket and lay down. I picked up one of the newspapers, *Kayhan*, and leafed through it. Finally I closed my eyes and drifted off to sleep.

I was rudely awakened by the telephone and politely reminded by the desk clerk that Captain Zand would be arriving in a half hour to pick me up. I shaved, showered, dressed in clean clothes and went down to the lobby just as the Mercedes—freshly washed and polished—pulled up outside. The bell captain and the same two assistants ushered me out and into the back seat beside Zand, who was alone except for the chauffeur. The captain's smile was pleasant enough, but the garlic on his breath almost made my eyes tear.

"You slept well, Dr. Frederickson?"

"Yup." It was true. For the first time since Neptune's death, I'd slept without dreams. While my grief for Neptune and concern for Garth were in no way diminished, another part of me had been revved up by the game in progress: I'd never heard the SAVAK accused of killing with kindness.

"Excellent. With your permission, we will have a light snack, then take a tour of the city."

"Sounds good. I'm hungry."

"You must try some of this garlic," Zand said, removing a jar from a large basket on the floor of the car. "This garlic has been aged for seven years; it does not leave a smell on the breath."

I glanced sideways to see if he was joking; he wasn't. I politely declined the garlic, mumbling something about an allergy, but I ate the rest of what was presented to me—thin, tender slices of cold chicken and fruit. While we ate, the driver expertly guided the car through the streets of Tehran.

"If you will be patient," the captain said, wiping his mouth with a linen napkin, "it will be my honor to show you the high points of our city." He hesitated a moment and his voice dropped in pitch. "I promise you that most of your questions will be answered later this evening."

"Will I find out what you've done with my brother?"

He laughed and shook his head. "I think this talk about a brother must be some kind of American joke."

Being completely powerless does have its compensations; for one thing, it saves a lot of arguing. The sleep had refreshed me, and I felt a good deal more relaxed than when I'd stepped off the plane. I leaned back in my seat and surveyed the exotic vista rolling by outside my window.

Once Zand asked me—in Farsi—if I spoke Farsi. I gave him a puzzled look. When he repeated the question in English, I answered no—except for the few simple words of greeting he'd already heard. He poured me a glass of strong brandy he called *arak*, then began a running dialogue on the passing sights. Zand was an excellent guide, with a thorough knowledge of the city.

The streets of Tehran were a strange, heady mixture of the old and new; young girls clad in the latest fashions from Rome, Paris or the United States walked side by side with older women who were draped in *chadors*, the traditional dark body shrouds. Everywhere, in even the smallest sidewalk shops, there were pictures of the Shah and the royal family. The Shah, his queen and their children looked the way any other family might look with a few hundred thousand dollars' worth of jewels jammed onto their fingers and sewn into their robes. Farah was beautiful, a fine-featured woman with hot eyes, high cheekbones and a full, sensuous mouth. The Crown Prince was handsome, with just a trace of an expression indicating that he occasionally found the whole Royal Family number a drag. I liked that.

The Shah himself, despite a crown which to my Western eye made him look slightly ridiculous, had tremendous presence. He seemed, well, *regal*; if there was such a thing as a kingly look, Pahlavi had it. His eyes were bright and intelligent, if cruel and incredibly arrogant. I didn't try to read anything else in the face; there was too much royal camouflage surrounding it.

The photographs covered the interiors of the shops like wallpaper, dominating everything, exuding a superficially benign but overwhelming ubiquity that I found humorous and sobering at the same time: Shah Mohammed Reza Pahlavi was obviously not a man to worry about overexposure. If an American President had arranged such a display, he'd have been laughed out of office. But this was not America, and the Shah was not the President; he was an all-powerful monarch whose reign depended, to at least some degree, on the quiet acceptance—indeed, worship—of his subjects. This was accomplished, in large part, by a masterly job of public relations and expert application of principles of group psychology. From the omnipresence of the photographs, it was easy to understand how the Iranian people could eventually come to mistake the man, woman and children for gods. It was an ancient technique that seemed to have lost none of its effectiveness down through the ages. Still I wondered how seriously all of this Royal Overkill was taken by the population; I thought it the better part of wisdom not to ask.

Zand finally ordered that the car be parked. We got out,

and I followed the man as he walked briskly under a canopy and down an alleyway into a city within a city. "This is the bazaar," he said quietly.

It was dirty and smelled of animals and unwashed humans, but its overall effect, seeping into the mind as the odors seeped into the nostrils, was fascinating. It was the ultimate marketplace, a conglomeration of bazaars within bazaars, the whole strung together over acres of land and covered by a rickety wooden canopy with exposed electric wiring that seemed ready to explode into flame at any moment. Everywhere we went, people stared at the sight of the tall army captain walking with the dwarf. I affected a studied air of unconcern.

We spent a good deal of time in the rug bazaar, with my host going on in great detail about the intricate weaving and dyeing procedures that made Persian carpets the finest in the world. I knew a little about Persian carpets and I said nothing; my mind was on the question of Garth's whereabouts and what the SAVAK was up to. Also, my appreciation of the carpets' beauty was tempered by the knowledge that many had been produced primarily by child labor, children having the only fingers small enough to perform the fine knotting techniques used for the finest rugs.

We spent another hour in the bazaar, then headed back to the car. It had grown dark, and the stars glittered diamond-hard in the black desert sky that covered the city like an ebony dome. Zand's running patter had sputtered to a halt, and we rode in silence up above the city to the slopes of one of the surrounding mountains. It seemed the captain considered his duties as guide discharged; he seemed more the military man again, tense, with a renewed sense of purpose.

The driver parked the car at the foot of a hill next to a flight of stone steps that led up to a large, gaily lighted restaurant. "We will wait here," Zand said evenly.

He got out; I followed and stood beside him. Below us,

Tehran was a sparkling sea of lights. The driver sat stiff and unmoving behind the wheel of the car, which was still running.

"Welcome to Iran, Dr. Frederickson."

As I turned in the direction of the deep, husky voice, the man who had spoken stepped out of the shadows. He was darker than Zand, with a head that seemed just a bit too small for his large shoulders and barrel chest. He had thick, wavy black hair and dense eyebrows that crawled across his brow like giant caterpillars; the eyebrows formed a striking contrast to the carefully tended, pencil-thin moustache on his lip. The eyes beneath the eyebrows were cold, dark and cunning, and his sunken cheeks made his face seem oddly skull-like. He spoke English with barely a trace of an accent.

Zand bowed. "Dr. Frederickson, I would like you to meet Colonel Bahman Arsenjani."

I shook the hand that was proffered; Arsenjani had fingers with the strength of steel cables. "I'm flattered at the attention," I said wryly. "Who's minding the SAVAK store while you're out here playing charades?"

Arsenjani's smile never touched his eyes. "Of course, in the circles you've been traveling in, it's only natural that you've heard my name bandied about."

"Of course. It seems you and your relatives are legends in your own time."

His lips parted and I caught a flash of gold. "How's your side?"

"Lots of wires and pins. I feel like an erector set." I hoped he wasn't thinking of taking me apart.

"But you're in working order; you heal quickly."

"And you get Grade A information."

The preliminary skirmishing over, Arsenjani motioned for me to follow him as he started up the steps toward the restaurant. His broad shoulders rolled beneath the fabric of his suit jacket. He reminded me of a classy version of Hassan

Khordad; everything about him smelled of control, discipline and ruthlessness. I was feeling a bit clammy.

We reached the top of the steps and I followed Arsenjani across a wide expanse of marble, past a row of white-clad waiters, to a large, luxuriously appointed table at the north end of the dining patio. Two waiters immediately sprang forward to pull out our chairs. Arsenjani motioned for me to sit down, then sat at the head of the table, to my left. Zand had remained behind.

"Now you will sample some of the finest cuisine in the world," Arsenjani said, snapping his fingers at the waiters. "I hope you don't mind; I've taken the liberty of ordering for both of us."

"Thanks. A condemned man's last meal?"

"I was told you had an odd sense of humor. I can assure you that Iran does not waste food like this on its enemies."

"Let's stop fucking around, Arsenjani. You've got me, so why not let Garth go?"

He looked at me for a long time without blinking. " 'Garth' is the name of your brother?"

"You know goddamn well it is."

"Captain Zand mentioned this curious obsession of yours concerning your brother, so I've checked the records. A Garth Frederickson did enter this country eighteen days ago as a tourist. Everything was in perfect order. My men are checking the hospital records at this very moment. Unless he's gone to the more remote areas of the country, it shouldn't take us long to find him, and then we'll see that you're reunited." He paused. "You don't believe me, do you?"

"You know I don't. How about an address for Neptune Tabrizi's family?"

He snapped his fingers. "The woman who was killed. *That's* why your brother came here! And you think—"

"God *damn* it, Arsenjani!" I hissed, bringing my fist crashing down on the table. I was immediately sorry; it would do me absolutely no good to lose my temper, and I mumbled an apology which I didn't feel but hoped might throw him off balance.

"You're really afraid, aren't you?" he asked quietly.

"Shitless. But I'm here for my brother. When do we stop this game and get down to business?"

Arsenjani's answer was a thin smile. I stared back at him. "Indulge me," he said at last. "You have nothing to fear, I assure you."

A sharp-eyed waiter with a limp appeared with a large basket of soft white bread and chilled crocks of pearl-gray caviar. I sipped at the small glass of chilled vodka that had come with it. "What happened to Parviz Maher?" I asked, made nervous by the silence.

The SAVAK chief slowly buttered a piece of bread, smeared a tiny mound of caviar over it. He nibbled at the bread, then set it down. He carefully wiped his moustache with an embossed linen napkin, then put a flame to a Winston cigarette. "Ah, yes," he said, picking at a stray piece of tobacco that had fallen on the spotless tablecloth. "You see, we regularly read Mr. Maher's mail. The codes Maher and his friends use are really quite simplistic. Mr. Maher's been frightened a bit, but that's all. Soon he'll be back running his silly errands for the Confederation of Iranian Students, but that's all right with us. How else could we keep track of what they're up to?"

"When are you going to stop jerking me around, Arsenjani?"

He reached across the table for a decanter, poured me a glass of wine, which I left untouched. I watched his eyes; they hadn't changed. Somehow, he reminded me of a cobra. "Iran is a warm, friendly country," he said, arching his caterpillar eyebrows. "Of *course* you're here because we wanted you here, but you are an honored guest in our country; the fact of the matter is that you've done His Majesty a great service."

"By killing three of your agents and knocking out a good part of your New York operation?"

Arsenjani smiled. "You killed Hassan Khordad and his lieutenants," he said evenly. "But there is a great deal that you don't understand. As I said, you have done His Majesty a great service and we simply wish to honor you." He raised his eyebrows again, this time inquiringly. I said nothing. "By the way," he continued, "how are Ali Azad and our dear friends who call themselves the Confederation of Iranian Students?"

"You'd know better than I would."

He clucked his tongue in distaste. "The C.I.S. are like spoiled children who must be slapped occasionally, but not taken seriously."

"Very gracious of you, especially in view of the fact that you know I'm supposed to be here working for them."

"Yes, but you're a professional; you came here looking for their hero, Mehdi Zahedi—and more important to you, it seems, your brother. No matter. I don't believe you have anything against the Shah."

"That's very charitable thinking for the head of the SAVAK. I'd like to think I was neutral."

"The idea of a king doesn't offend you?"

"I won't deny that I'm partial to governments which allow the governed some say over their lives."

"Do you believe *Americans* have any real control over their lives? Now *you* are—what was that quaint saying?— 'jerking me around'?"

Ignoring the laughter in his voice, I looked over his shoulder; beyond the walls of the terrace, Tehran gleamed in the distance like a child's electric toy, close enough to touch. "Form is important, even when there isn't much substance."

"Perhaps the Americans are better suited temperamentally to a representative government than, say, Iranians."

"I've heard that argument before."

"Hearing an argument, no matter how many times, is not in itself a refutation of that argument."

"Whatever you say." I didn't feel up to a round of word games.

Arsenjani traced a pattern on the tablecloth with a thick, well-manicured fingernail. "Would you be unhappy if I told you that you may have saved the Shahanshah's life?"

"I'd be surprised. What are you talking about?"

"In good time," he said slowly. "First, I wish to speak to you of a . . . sensitive matter."

"I'm not sure you'll be doing me a favor."

Arsenjani ignored me. "No one knows better than I that His Majesty has not always been a good ruler, or even a good man. Indeed, as a young man installed on his father's throne by mercenary foreign powers, he was positively inept; that, of course, was exactly what the Western powers wanted."

The waiter with a limp reappeared with more wine, re-filled our glasses, shuffled away.

"I speak to you like this," Arsenjani continued when the man was out of hearing, "because I want you to know that I am sincere in what I say. I assume Ali Azad has babbled to you about the great Mossadegh regime?"

"He mentioned Mossadegh."

Arsenjani ground out his cigarette. The waiter immediately appeared with a clean ashtray, and Arsenjani lighted another. "The present Shah, when he came to power, had no knowledge of what it takes to rule a country; he had no social mission, no sense of duty. Later, he was thrown out of power and humiliated by Mossadegh and Parliament, with the support of the people." He paused and blew smoke over our heads. "Now, it is important for you to understand that the Shah was not, and *is* not, a stupid man. He was badly shaken by those events. Their lesson was not lost on him."

"Mossadegh didn't last long," I said. "And he didn't go out of his own accord."

Arsenjani again shrugged his massive shoulders. "It's true that the Shah could not have returned to power without the help of the Americans. But I ask you to look at the record since then. It's very doubtful that Mossadegh would have been able to do as much, for the simple reason that by nationalizing the oil industry, he cut himself off from most sources of foreign aid."

"We'll never know what Mossadegh would have been able to do, will we? He wasn't given any time."

Arsenjani snorted disdainfully. "The Shah's program of land reform, his 'White Revolution,' is unparalleled. The literacy rate has doubled in the last decade. Today the Shah is more than a man who rules only because his father ruled. He's an urbane, educated man who cares deeply about his country and his people."

"I'm told the people here cared deeply about Mossadegh."

"The Shah is a greater man than Mossadegh *ever* was," the SAVAK chief said forcefully. There was a slight flush around his cheeks. "And what an underdeveloped country needs more than anything else *is* a great man. Again I offer you the example of your own country, which seems to survive despite, rather than because of, the men you elect to run it. Someday, perhaps, Iran may be that strong. But that time has not yet come; there are simply too many problems that can be solved only through efficient, autocratic means. The Shah takes care of the affairs of state, and it is the job of men like me to make certain that he remains in power to do it."

"Spoken like a true patriot, at length and with conviction."

He didn't smile. "I am quite serious; I feel that what I say is obvious." More food came, and Arsenjani gestured out over the expanse of the table. "Eat while it is hot."

We helped ourselves from platters of steaming rice topped with braised lamb, tomatoes and onions. "You've been very patient, Frederickson," Arsenjani said between mouthfuls.

"I was afraid you'd never notice. You said something about saving the Shah's life."

He swallowed a chunk of lamb, sipped more wine, nodded. "It's quite possible."

"By killing Hassan Khordad?"

"Correct. You saved us the trouble." He took another chunk of lamb into his mouth, then closed his eyes, savoring it. I watched the pieces work their way down his throat. "Khordad wasn't working for us, as you supposed," he continued, sipping more wine. He suddenly set his glass down hard. His eyes flashed. "In fact, Khordad was a key member of a very dangerous organization sometimes referred to as GEM. You've heard of them?"

"I've heard of them," I said, frowning. If it was a ploy, it was a good one, and I couldn't think of a thing to say. My mind raced back over the events of the past few weeks, trying to sort out the facts and see if they could be rearranged to say what Arsenjani claimed they said, but I was having difficulty concentrating. "The facts—"

"Your problem is that you started off with a basic assumption that was incorrect," Arsenjani interrupted gently. "Once you concluded that Khordad was a SAVAK agent, everything seemed to fall into place. In fact, the exact opposite was true—which is why we're sharing this delightful dinner. We take GEM very seriously; Hassan Khordad was a dangerous revolutionary, and his death was a blessing to us." He hesitated, then added, "A mixed blessing, perhaps. Actually, we were hopeful that he would lead us to the top organizers before you, uh, descended on him and his gunrunning colleagues."

"The import-export company was a front for the gun smuggling?"

"Correct. *That* we discovered only recently, and we were about to move in on them in any case."

"For a GEM agent, Orrin Bannon seemed incredibly pro-Shah."

The SAVAK chief laughed. "Do you believe that an American who was *anti*-Shah would be able to get an import-export license from us? He had a good act. In any case, Bannon was a very low-level operative—an employee, really, who worked for money. Only Iranians actually belong to GEM; as far as we know, Khordad was the only contact Bannon ever met. You must have made him *very* nervous when you started asking questions about Khordad."

"To say the least."

"Khordad operated in *this* country for many years. We found out about him, but GEM got him out of the country a step ahead of us. He traveled for a few months, then finally ended up with what he thought was a safe cover with the same circus you used to work for. I believe you were known then as Mongo the Magnificent; among your friends, the name has stuck with you."

"I'll bet you know the color of my bathroom walls."

"No, but I haven't had time to review this week's report," Arsenjani said smugly. "Anyway, GEM's activities in your country are more, shall we say, theoretical and organizational. With Khordad, they suddenly had one of their own killers on their hands and weren't quite sure what to do with him."

"You're saying it was GEM that was responsible for Neptune Tabrizi's death?"

"Correct, inasmuch as GEM was responsible for Khordad's running amok in the United States."

"Why *was* Khordad running amok?"

"Ah," Arsenjani said, pressing the tips of his fingers together. "Now our information becomes a little vague. I was hoping *you* might be able to enlighten *us* in this area."

Another surprise. "It had something to do with Mehdi Zahedi's disappearing. I think Khordad's job was to keep anyone from finding out who Zahedi was, or where he'd gone."

"Of course." He cleared his throat. "I don't suppose *you* know where Zahedi is?"

The question was so unusual that it shocked me into realizing that Arsenjani's voice and mannerisms, combined with jet lag and Persian wine, were having what amounted to a hypnotic effect. I was still a stranger a long way from home, enmeshed in some very devious business, being asked to play pawn to someone else's major pieces. It was time for the pawn to back off a bit, which made it my turn to laugh. "Did you bring me up here to pump me?"

"On the contrary, I seem to be the one doing most of the talking; I assure you we don't need you as an informer, and I would never insult a guest by asking him to volunteer information he didn't want to divulge."

Arsenjani, wearing a pained expression, paused to let me speak. He was not a man I would underestimate.

"How did Khordad get involved with Zahedi in the first place?" I said.

"Is it not obvious? The leadership must have saddled poor Zahedi with the thankless task of acting as Khordad's controller. Now, if we only knew where Zahedi went in such a hurry, we might finally have a line on the leaders' identities."

"And no one in the Confederation of Iranian Students knows *anything* about this?"

Arsenjani laid his palms flat on the table. "Zahedi was a top professional in an ultrasecret terrorist organization. *He* knew we have informers in the Confederation, even if Ali doesn't. And Zahedi is very clever; he thought that if he made enough noise we wouldn't take him any more seriously than we do the rest of those idiot students. Of course, he was wrong; we've been aware of his GEM activities for almost a year."

"What was his role in GEM?"

"Anti-Shah propagandist was his obvious role, but we also believe he was a GEM recruiter."

"He never tried to recruit Ali."

Arsenjani smiled. "Would *you*? No, Zahedi was recruiting professional mercenaries for actual fighting."

"Aren't you worried that I might tell Ali he has informers in his organization?"

Arsenjani shrugged broadly. "It wouldn't make any difference. The information would only set them all to squabbling among themselves, and that would serve the SAVAK's purpose."

"You haven't killed Zahedi?"

"Not yet," he said softly.

"You know I think Zahedi's here in Iran. You're telling me that if he is, you don't know where?"

Arsenjani laughed sharply. "Ah, I only wish I did. Finding Zahedi would make my life a good deal easier. At the least, it would assure me a larger cottage on the Caspian."

"Why didn't you have him assassinated when you had the chance?"

"Frankly, it's now obvious we should have. As I said, our hope was that he'd eventually lead us to the main organizers. Now it is *most* important that we find out where he is and why he left."

"I can understand that," I said. "If he was warned that you were on to him, it means that GEM has infiltrated the SAVAK."

He gave a single, perfunctory nod of his head; he looked very uncomfortable. One thing was unequivocally certain: GEM was making Arsenjani's, not to mention the Shah's, head spin.

I leaned forward on the table and watched his face as I said, "Who's Nasser Razvan?"

Arsenjani seemed happy that I'd changed the subject. He gave what appeared to be an appreciative nod, reached into his pocket and removed a maroon Iranian passport, which he laid on the table in front of me. "Nasser is one of our most talented agents. It was Nasser who uncovered the fact that Mehdi Zahedi is a GEM operative. Also, we believe Nasser is very close to unmasking the top leadership."

I opened the passport and studied the photograph; it showed a dark-skinned man with high cheekbones. The writing, in both French and Farsi, identified the man as Nasser Razvan. "He looks like an American black," I said as I handed the passport back.

"And he can speak like a resident of one of your ghettos, which is precisely what makes him so valuable. Actually, he's a Bakhtiari tribesman, but no one who didn't know would ever guess it. Nasser worked as a laboratory assistant at your university."

"If Razvan was so close, why did he pull up stakes and fly back here?"

"We'd captured a GEM agent we had reason to believe was top-echelon—"

"Firouz Maleki." The name in Khordad's notebook.

"That's right. Maleki would certainly have been able to tell us what we wanted to know, and we wanted Nasser here when we interrogated him. After all, he was our top American agent." Arsenjani's eyes grew opaque. "Unfortunately, Maleki died before we could complete our interrogation."

"How did he die?"

He glanced up at me sharply. "That's being investigated."

"I'll bet it is. You're thinking that one of his own terrorist friends may have helped him make a painless exit: the question of GEM in the SAVAK again."

"Perhaps," Arsenjani said tightly.

"Why tell me all this?"

"Because GEM, through Khordad, killed your brother's mistress; we want to destroy GEM. It would seem we have a common interest."

"You want me to work for the *SAVAK*?"

"Does that offend you? There are many unresolved questions in this matter that you could help unravel."

"I'll give it some thought," I lied. "You say you don't know where Mehdi Zahedi is. Do you know that's not his real name?"

"It's a *nom de guerre*. Not being able to learn his real identity has been a major handicap."

"Why do you suppose Zahedi disappeared on the same day your agent flew back to Iran?"

"*That* is one of the unresolved questions I was hoping you might have an answer to."

"I don't."

Arsenjani lighted yet another cigarette and studied me through a cloud of blue-white smoke. "It would seem Zahedi somehow found out about Nasser, panicked and ran. It's very distressing to the SAVAK when a top agent's cover is blown so quickly and thoroughly."

"Then you haven't sent Razvan back yet?"

He shook his head. "And valuable time is being lost." He paused, sighed. "The fools would even destroy Persepolis."

"Why should they want to do that?"

"Persepolis is more than just another pile of ruins. It's a symbol, the very epicenter of our civilization. It's the crowning jewel of what was once the Persian Empire. Persepolis represents powerful memories; sometimes, memories are all that hold a people together."

"Persepolis also represents the monarchy."

"Precisely. Its destruction could have great symbolic

meaning to our people. It's also an excellent hiding place, with a vast network of underground water channels. They planned to kill the Shah during last year's Shiraz art festival. Fortunately, we uncovered the plot and, in February, were finally able to capture Maleki. Just in time, I might add."

"Zahedi took off near the end of February. Maybe he found out you'd captured Maleki. He knew you could make him talk. Suddenly he found himself in a very vulnerable position."

"We *must* determine if GEM has infiltrated SAVAK," Arsenjani said to himself. He glanced up and reddened, apparently embarrassed by his own intensity. "But that is my problem."

"It would be *my* problem if I started working for you. You know, it's *still* possible that Zahedi's here."

"Anything's possible, but I doubt it—especially if he knows we're on to him. If he is here, we'll eventually track him down."

The napkin I'd been arranging into a smooth pyramid fell when I took my hand away. "What am I supposed to tell Ali when I get back? He still thinks he paid for this trip."

Arsenjani spread his hands on the table. "I'm sure you can make up a story. If you prefer not to, *tell* him Zahedi is a GEM agent; tell him we know everything he does." Arsenjani abruptly leaned forward. "When you report back to Ali, you'll put the fear of God into him. We know *everything* he does, everyone he talks to; he'll know he can't fart without our smelling it."

"You underestimate Ali," I said evenly. "He's too passionate, but he's intelligent. Iran could use him."

"Then you tell him to return here and bring his skills back to where they're needed. Tell him to stop his nonsense and return to help us build a better country for our people."

"No reprisals?"

"No reprisals. You have my personal word on that." Now he leaned back in his chair. He looked rather satisfied with himself. "Is there anything else you'd like to know?"

"Yeah. Where have you got Garth?"

Jet lag and wine again; it was absolutely the wrong thing to say, the wrong attitude to take. The self-satisfied smile on Arsenjani's face froze, then turned ugly. "You're a fool. Now you will come with me, please."

11

IT LOOKED AS THOUGH I'd worn out my welcome; Arsenjani, without another word, rose and stiffly descended the stone steps to the car. I followed and got into the back, as before, but Arsenjani slid into the front seat beside the chauffeur. Cut off from any conversation by a glass partition, I leaned back in the rich-smelling leather vastness of the back seat and tried to relax; the car felt like a tomb.

A half hour later the car braked to a stop. I looked out the small opera window and was surprised to find that we seemed to be in the middle of the city, in front of a building that announced in both French and Farsi, BANK *MELI*. Across the street, barely discernible in the moonlight shadows, two soldiers with submachine guns stood stiffly at attention. The facade of the bank was shrouded in darkness, except for a single dimly lighted doorway on the left.

The glass partition in the car rolled down. "Go into the building through the lighted doorway, Frederickson," Arsenjani said. "The car and driver will be waiting for you when you come out. I will not; I won't be seeing you again." He slowly turned around in his seat and fixed me with his eyes, which now seemed cold, hard, almost luminous. "I *hope* I won't be seeing you again."

"Who's inside the building, Arsenjani?"

"No more questions. Go." The partition whizzed up, ominously punctuating the SAVAK chief's sentence.

Very conscious of the gunmen, I slipped out of the car and walked the twenty yards to the lighted doorway. I walked past another grim-faced guard, down a long corridor and through a massive armored door that had obviously been left open for me. I found myself in a huge chamber that shimmered with bright light. It took a few moments to become accustomed to the glare, and then I felt my stomach muscles tighten when I realized where I was.

The room was crowded with long rows of glass display cases. Inside the cases were dozens of gold, jewel-encrusted crowns and daggers; platters piled high with emeralds, topazes, opals, diamonds. I was looking at the most fabulous collection of treasure in the world—the Crown Jewels of Iran.

I heard footsteps behind me, wheeled and involuntarily took a step backward when I recognized one of the few remaining total rulers on earth. The Shah of Iran, Mohammed Reza Pahlavi, was wearing a beige cashmere sport jacket, gray turtleneck and matching slacks, black shoes; except for blurred photographs taken on Swiss ski slopes, it was the first time I'd ever seen him outside a military uniform with a chestful of medals. He was shorter than I'd imagined, but oddly enough he seemed even more regal in civilian clothes, removed from the trappings of crowns, jewels and robes; he was a man who obviously took the king business seriously. He wasn't tall, but he had an electric, commanding presence, with sharp facial features. His hair was white and wavy, in sharp contrast to his piercing black eyes and eyebrows. He had the ruddy, weathered complexion of an outdoor sportsman and—as if to reassure me that even Shahs are human—a razor nick on his chin.

Human, maybe; but one casual cough from the man and Garth, I, or anyone else he didn't fancy would be dead. Fencing with Arsenjani was one thing, playing with Himself quite another. He—or his naked power—frightened me, and I was going to be very careful of what I said.

He walked quickly forward, lightly pressed his fingertips together. "Welcome to Iran, Dr. Frederickson. Or may I call you Mongo?"

"You may call me anything you like, Your, er, Majesty."

He looked at me oddly for a moment, then abruptly shoved his hands into his pockets and began to pace back and forth in front of one of the cases; the pacing was not nervous, but the casual—indeed, elegant—lope of a thoughtful man who knew he was completely in charge. "You've performed a number of times at Rainier's Monaco Circus Festival. You are an incredibly gifted man, and I mean that in every sense of the word."

I heard myself clearing my throat. "Thank you, Your Majesty."

"Impressive, isn't it?" he said, abruptly changing the subject and indicating the room with a grand sweep of his arm.

"Uh, yes, Your Majesty. 'Impressive' might be one way of putting it."

He smiled easily. "There are some who'll tell you that it's all paste, that I've spirited the real jewels away to secret vaults in Zurich. It's not true, you know. Everything you see here is authentic; the jewels form the backing for our currency."

"I'd have thought you had enough oil to take care of that." The Shah wanted to chat: I'd chat.

Pahlavi shook his head impatiently. "One day the oil will run out; thirty, fifty, one hundred years from now, and it will be gone. If we are not a completely industrialized nation by

159

then, self-sufficient and independent of our oil revenues, we will again be nothing more than a *once*-great nation that other countries make sport of. I intend to make certain that does not happen." He paused, touched his forehead, added distantly, "It's hard being king."

I looked into his face to see if he was joking. He most definitely was not.

"This country is *my* responsibility, Dr. Frederickson," he continued, apparently seeing something in my face he didn't like. "Mine *alone*. There is no one else to *responsibly* look after it. Can you understand that?"

"Uh, I certainly can."

Something in my voice must not have rung true. "You don't think much of kings, do you?" he asked, a slight, angry tremor in his voice. "I assume you find someone like me faintly . . . *ridiculous*?"

"On the contrary, Your Majesty: I find you most impressive.

"Ah," he intoned, half-raising one regal, impeccably manicured hand, "but you've made certain moral judgments. Tell me: why do you assume somebody like Mehdi Zahedi or any one of the other GEM thugs can do more for Iran than I can? These people would bring chaos, I assure you."

The point. It seemed the pawn was being given the royal treatment by the biggest major piece of all, the only piece that really counted. It made the pawn very curious. Others could argue, as I'd heard them do, whether or not the Shah of Iran was the ultimate existentialist hero; a self-made man who'd become an enlightened king, not because he had to, but because he wanted to. To me, at the moment, he was simply the most dangerous enemy I'd ever faced.

"Consider the possibility that GEM could cause enough upheaval to allow the Russians to move in," the Shah continued. "They would, you know, given half a chance.

They've tried it before, in the north. Would Iran be better off as a Russian satellite?"

"I'm sure not, Your Majesty," I said quietly.

"GEM means to kill me."

"I know, Your Majesty."

He looked at me sharply. "Understand: I am not *personally* afraid for my life; I am prepared to die at any time. But my death would be a tragedy for Iran. I *must* remain alive in order to lead Iran to its rightful place as a leading world power. Iran needs me; my people need me."

"Uh, excuse me, Your Majesty, but I don't quite see what all of this has to do with me."

Mohammed Reza Pahlavi removed a key from his jacket pocket and inserted it into the lock on one of the glass cases. Immediately the silence was shattered by an alarm. The Shah snapped his fingers; the guard in the room with us ran out of the chamber, and a moment later the alarm was shut off. The Shah opened the case and removed a huge diamond from a tray filled with more than a hundred. He held it up between his thumb and forefinger. "I believe that when this unpleasantness is over you will find, like most people, that you have developed an attachment for Iran—our magnificent culture, and our way of life. Perhaps you might even care to . . . represent . . . Iran in some capacity."

In the silence I imagined I could hear my heart beating. "I'm sorry, sir," I said carefully, watching him. "The main reason I came here was to search for my brother. I haven't found him yet."

"And you think your brother is here?"

"Colonel Arsenjani confirmed that he entered the country."

"If your brother is here, then Arsenjani will find him for you," he said impatiently. "It is not a problem."

"It is for me," I said evenly. "Until I know he's safe, I can't concentrate on anything else."

"But you might be able to concentrate on . . . other things . . . if you were to find your brother?"

"Yes," I said quickly.

The Shah stared at me for what seemed a long time, then unexpectedly broke into a smile which revealed absolutely nothing. "Then we can only hope that you find him soon. Perhaps by now he's already back in the United States."

"Perhaps."

"It's been a pleasure meeting you, Dr. Frederickson," he said abruptly. "Your car is waiting for you, and I've assigned a guide for the duration of your visit. Please consider our country to be your own."

"Thank you, Your Majesty. Do you think there's a possibility that my brother might show up if I wait here long enough?"

"I'm sure you understand I cannot bother myself with such trivial details. These things are taken care of by the SAVAK. Of course, you should do what you believe to be in your brother's interest . . . and your own. Goodbye."

With that, the Shah brushed past me and walked quickly from the room. Although I was only a few seconds behind him, his entourage was already gone by the time I left the bank. The guards were gone, and the lights in the bank blinked off as I reached the sidewalk. There was a heavy grinding sound, then a bang as the vault door was closed and sealed. I got into the car and gave the driver directions to take me back to my hotel.

Even with my massive ego, I had serious doubts that I could be of any real use to Iran, in the United States or anywhere else; yet the Shah himself, if only as a sort of regal self-amusement, had seen fit to step in and make a kind of offer. Also, Arsenjani had told at least one big whopper: the leaders of GEM might be many things, but no one had accused them of stupidity; it would be sheer insanity for them to try to hide Khordad in a circus when the owner was obviously hyping him into a headliner with a major publicity campaign in every city. The deadly, maddening game continued, and I was getting tired of being treated like the village idiot.

12

NEW YORK CITY, like Los Angeles, was the home of some of the most skillful liars in the world, and I'd met more than my share. Arsenjani was a master liar, but not the champ by any means. And I was bothered by more than the obvious fallacy of GEM's trying to hide Khordad in a circus. Like those of any talented liar, Arsenjani's lies were undoubtedly laced with large doses of truth. At the moment it was impossible for me to tell which was which, but it was enough for me to know he was lying. The evening's bizarre exercise had been designed to make me *think* I was potentially invaluable to the Shah and SAVAK. I considered that nonsense. Also, as angry as Garth had been, as heartsick, he would never willingly have overstayed a planned visit to Iran without finally contacting me—precisely because he knew I'd come after him, even if it meant my death. The SAVAK had known it too; I was still convinced they had him. Maybe they'd let him go if I went back to the United States, maybe they wouldn't; maybe I'd already been programmed for whatever charade the SAVAK was playing, and Garth was dead. In any case, I wasn't about to sit around and depend on the good graces of the SAVAK. It seemed to me that my best option was to go back to basics and hope to find the secret square. It was time to force the issue.

The next morning, I discovered that Arsenjani didn't want me doing any comparative shopping for an alternative to his story. I'd picked up a tail. It was nothing serious; he was a small man with scuffed brown shoes and a worn, shiny suit that would no longer take a press. He kept his face hidden behind a newspaper which he held too high, and he never turned the pages; I doubted whether he'd be able to follow a train if he were riding in the caboose. He looked like one of Arsenjani's jokes, a not-so-subtle reminder that the SAVAK chief was unhappy with the idea of me running around the game board by myself.

I sat down in a chair in the lobby and let my mind wander through the labyrinth of possibilities. The obvious presence of the shadow seemed a strange move which could be a simple blunder by the spy chief, or a dangerous gambit. The man in the shiny suit was probably a decoy. When I lost him, their real ace would go into action. And my going to the trouble of losing him would be an admission that this particular pawn was on the move, trying to take control of the game.

I already had a tension headache. I bought a bottle of aspirin and went back up to my room, where I stretched out on the bed and began thumbing through *Kayhan*. I found it a surprisingly good newspaper, sophisticated and cosmopolitan. There were no articles criticizing the Shah, to be sure, but there was no gross propagandizing either.

I suddenly stopped skimming when I came to a classified section listing a number of English-speaking individuals offering their services as tour guides. There was one girl's name that looked distinctly American, and I circled it: Kathy Martin. I wanted something more than the "official" tour.

There was a number. I dialed it and spoke to a bright, intelligent voice with just a trace of an Irish accent. She was available. I gave her a story about being a visiting professor, and we made arrangements to meet at the north end of the bazaar in the morning. I doubted Arsenjani would hold anything against a person I'd so obviously picked at random from the newspaper.

The next morning I rose early, dressed casually and draped a camera bag over my shoulder before going down into the lobby. I walked out the doors without looking back. I didn't have to look to know that the man with the shiny suit was standing next to a newspaper kiosk; I wondered if he'd been there all night.

I spent a few minutes strolling around, looking into the shop windows and pointing my camera at some of the more exotic sights. I bought a few small items, then hailed a taxi, allowing my shadow plenty of time to find one of his own. I knew I was walking on eggs and didn't want the other man to have the slightest suspicion that I knew I was being tailed. Considering his incompetence, that could prove to be a difficult job; I was afraid I might have to start crawling on all fours. When I did lose him, it would have to look like a thoroughly convincing accident.

After giving the driver directions in passable Farsi, I settled back in my seat and took a series of deep breaths, trying to relax. I got off at the east end of the bazaar, walked around for fifteen minutes, then slipped my companion in a bona fide crowd scene. When I was sure I'd lost any backup man who might be trailing the action, I doubled back through the bazaar and came out at the north end.

Kathy Martin was immediately recognizable. She was standing near a soft-drink stand talking animatedly with a group of young Iranians. I put her age at around twenty; her skin was very light and freckled, and her wheat-colored hair was tied back in a pony tail held in place with a red plaid scarf. Her trim body was clad in jeans and a denim work shirt; the overall effect was one of femininity and vulnerability. I wondered how she'd ended up in Iran.

I went over and introduced myself. The frailty of her body was offset by the green, liquid fire of her eyes.

"*You're* Dr. Frederickson?" It was the exclamation of a child, not intended to insult or hurt. Immediately she flushed and put her hand to her mouth. "Oh, I'm terribly sorry."

After smiling to show that all was forgiven, I shifted the conversation to a more professional bent. "How's your Farsi?" She started to rattle on in Farsi, much too fast for me to follow. "Okay," I said, raising my hands in surrender, "you'll do."

She grinned back, showing even white teeth. "I read and write, too."

The attractive blonde and the dwarf were beginning to attract attention, and attention was something we could do without. I suggested we discuss our business over tea.

We crossed the street and walked a few blocks until we found one of the small, ubiquitous *chai* houses. We sat at a table near the rear and ordered two cups of the aromatic Iranian tea. She didn't seem to mind talking about herself, and I didn't mind listening. Her father was a well-known Iranologist. She attended the University of Tehran and spent summers guiding tourists while her father worked around the country at various archaeological digs; she'd spent most of her life in Iran, returning to the United States at regular intervals, but preferring the quiet, firm order of Iran to the seemingly incessant turmoil of her homeland. She was extremely pro-Shah, and doubted that Iran could accomplish anything without him. I listened to her political views and commented on her slight Irish brogue. She sounded pleased to discover that she still had it.

167

"Kathy," I said during a lull in the conversation, "I need a translator who's willing to travel a bit. I'm a gentleman at all times, and I'll pay your going wage, plus expenses."

"Where do you want to go?"

"Persepolis."

Her pony tail bobbed around her shoulders as she nodded enthusiastically. "Oh, you'll *love* Persepolis! There's nothing else like it in the world!"

"So I've heard. Can we get there by car?"

"Sure, but it's hard driving through a lot of desert. It's not at all like in the States." She paused and thoughtfully ran a pretty finger around the rim of her cup. "Also, there's something you should know about Iranian drivers. They're very—"

"I like deserts, and New York taxi drivers are the worst in the world."

Kathy arched a pale eyebrow; it looked like a warning. "We can go by plane much easier if you have the money."

Money was no problem; the fact that Arsenjani's men would undoubtedly be watching the airport was. "I prefer a car; that is, if you don't mind cars."

"Are you kidding? I don't like *planes*."

"Fine. How far is it?"

"About seven hundred kilometers to the south. It's a good nine-hour drive."

"Any place between here and there we can stop and rest?"

"Oh, I should say so. Persepolis is a few kilometers south of Shiraz, and Esfahan is about halfway. You'll love Esfahan too." Kathy was certainly not lacking for enthusiasm, or anything else as far as I could see. She swallowed and shook her head forcefully. "But I *must* tell you that the drivers are—"

"I want to see some of the countryside," I interrupted. "Don't worry; I'm a good driver."

"*Well*," she sighed, clapping her hands together in a gesture that could have been either enthusiasm or resignation, I'm game if you are."

I wrote out three hundred dollars' worth of traveler's checks and gave them to her, along with a list of items. "If you don't mind, I'd like you to pick up these things for me, along with a small, light suitcase. Also, if you would, rent the car. Keep what's left over as an advance. Okay?"

"Okay," she said, looking at the list. On her open face I could see her wondering why I didn't do my own shopping, but she didn't ask questions.

"Good. I'll meet you here tomorrow morning, same time. And there's one more thing I'd like you to do for me." I wrote down the names *Nasser Razvan, Mehdi Zahedi* as a flyer, *Firouz Maleki, Tabrizi*, and handed the list to her. "I'd like you to look in the Tehran directory and see if you can find any of these names. If so, write down the addresses."

She glanced at the list. "There are probably dozens of Tabrizis," she said. "It's a common name."

"All right," I said reluctantly, "cross that one off." There was no certainty Neptune's family lived in Tehran, no time to go traipsing around, and I was certain Garth wouldn't be with them anyway.

Kathy stared at me for a few moments, her smile slowly fading. "I hope you're not involved in anything illegal, Dr. Frederickson."

The question startled me. "No," I said evenly. "What could possibly be illegal about looking up some names?"

"Nothing," she said, shaking her head. "But you must remember that Iran is not the United States. People here do not do things that even *appear* unusual. The SAVAK is everywhere."

"Okay, Kathy," I said, deciding that a little paranoia is a healthy thing to have in a police state, "I'll bear that in mind."

I'd originally planned to leave my things behind in my room as a smoke screen, but I changed my mind. It didn't seem to serve any purpose; once I was gone, Arsenjani would certainly know it. Besides, up to that point I hadn't done anything overtly suspicious, and I wanted to keep it that way.

The next morning I packed and went down to the hotel's breakfast room. There'd been a changing of the guard; I picked the tall, swarthy man at a corner table, but it could just as easily have been the fat man who'd just risen and was paying his bill. It was probably both. I ate leisurely, then picked up my suitcase and went to the front desk. The desk clerk, with his expensive toupee and capped teeth, looked like a moonlighting actor.

"I'd like to pay my bill."

The clerk quickly leafed through his ledger, then glanced up and flashed a pound or so of shiny porcelain. "Your bill will be taken care of, Dr. Frederickson. Are you returning home?"

"No, I thought I'd get out and see a bit of the country."

"I'll call for your guide," he said, reaching for a telephone.

"No, thank you," I said with what I hoped was just the right amount of firmness. "I prefer traveling on my own."

"Very well," he said, looking slightly worried as he replaced the receiver. "Where will you be going?"

"Oh, I thought I'd head north."

"Ah, the Caspian! It is wonderful this time of year! Be sure to try the caviar; it's fresher there."

"I wouldn't miss it."

"May I call you a taxi?"

"No, thanks. I'm traveling light, and I'd like to walk around a bit. I'll catch a taxi to the airport later."

"Enjoy your trip, sir."

I walked quickly from the hotel. This time my tail, whoever he or she might be, was a top professional. Still, I could feel his presence and I knew that Arsenjani wasn't likely to buy two crowd scenes in a row. This time the break would have to be complete, and I wasted no time. Five minutes from the hotel I ducked into an alleyway, sprinted down it, went into a shop and exited through the front door. Ten minutes later, just to make certain, I repeated the same maneuver before heading for the bazaar.

Kathy was waiting for me in a Peykan, a bulky car that consisted of an Iranian-made frame with a Mercedes-Benz engine. "It looks good," I said with only a slight trace of skepticism, "but will it run?"

"Definitely, O Master," she said with a wide grin. "It's not pretty, but it's sturdy and dependable—the best thing for the desert."

"I'll take your word for it," I said, sliding in behind the wheel and pulling the seat all the way up before turning on the ignition.

"Dr. Frederickson," Kathy said uneasily, "I'll be happy to drive—if you want me to?"

"Do dwarf motorists make you uneasy?" I asked gently.

"Oh, *no*, sir," she exclaimed, flushing. "You just don't *understand!*"

"I like to drive. How did you make out with those names I gave you?"

"I'm sorry, sir. None of the names were listed."

Somehow I felt that Nasser Razvan, if he really was a member of the SAVAK, should have been, regardless of where he'd been operating for the past year or so. But I wasn't really surprised. As I pulled out into the traffic, Kathy tensed. Her hands went to her mouth and her face became almost bloodless. I wondered why.

13

It DIDN'T TAKE LONG for me to discover the reason for Kathy's disquiet; driving in Tehran was strictly a question of survival. It took less than a minute at this time of day to find that Tehran's only rules of the road could be equally applicable to trench warfare. Drivers bore down on me from *both* sides of the street; I watched a car passing another car, both of these cars passing a third which had wandered over onto the wrong side of a double line. Red lights seemed to serve primarily as a casual warning that there might be cars coming through an intersection. The behavior of the average motorist at any red light was to slow down, then inch out into the path of the oncoming cars until one driver lost his nerve and let the other driver through. Throughout the city, it seemed, driving was one prolonged game of Tehran Chicken. I tried to think of something witty to say, but it came out through clenched teeth as a kind of hysterical cackle.

"It's *strange*," Kathy murmured through her own clenched teeth. "On the one hand, Iranians are the most courteous and hospitable people in the world—that is, when they're dealing with you on a personal basis. On the road, at the wheel of a machine, they're not to be believed. Most of the American companies here forbid their executives to drive at all anywhere in Iran. You can see why."

"Yup," I said tightly. It seemed an incredibly sane policy. I would have added a few other things, but I was too busy dodging cars. Two Peykans were crumpled into each other in the opposite lane, halting all traffic while their drivers slugged away at each other.

"But there's a tension underneath all that courtesy," Kathy continued thoughtfully. "You can feel it. I guess they build up a lot of frustration opening doors for each other. A car's so *impersonal*; I suppose they take out all their anger on each other when they get in one."

Crazy sociology, but probably true. I nodded my head and mumbled something unintelligible as I continued my life-and-death struggle to get out of the city.

Forty-five minutes later we were on the outskirts of Tehran. Ahead of us, stretching south to the horizon, was the desert. I immediately felt an almost overwhelming sense of isolation; we'd been cast adrift from the cosmopolitan battleship of Tehran in a small, four-wheeled raft on a hot ocean of desert where time seemed to run backward. Kathy, for all her experience, seemed to sense this too. She was hunched down in her seat, hands clasped tightly in her lap as she stared out the window at the wasteland of mountains and sand, a devil's playground with its own very special kind of barren, deadly beauty.

I was suddenly very conscious of the car; the desert was no place to break down, and the hum of the motor, the orchestrated jangle of thousands of moving parts, became magnified and took on special meaning.

"I have a friend who's a soldier in the army," Kathy said quietly, not taking her eyes off the alien world outside. "Twice a year they go out into the desert for maneuvers.

Once, near here, some of the jeeps bogged down about three kilometers off the road. The men got out and walked another kilometer, but that was as far as they could go. There are places out there where the sand will suck a man right under."

I thought she would say more, but she didn't. I kept my eyes on the narrow, winding road ahead. The desert had thrown a cloak around both of us—a sudden, sharp reminder that life in many areas of the earth is constantly lived in the shadow of death. I remembered the music of the santur.

Kathy's mood lifted when we reached Ghom, a small city about halfway on the road to Esfahan. She sat up straight and pointed to the crowds of women in *chadors*. "This is a very holy city," she said, sounding like a tourist guide. "The Moslem holy men used to literally stone tourists; that is, when they weren't spitting on them or kicking them."

"Very holy of them."

Kathy laughed politely. "Ghom was a very dangerous place for foreigners, even *Moslem* foreigners. That was bad for tourism, so the Shah decided to do something about it. The holy men, naturally, opposed him. One night the Shah sent in a hundred of his best troops to beat up all the holy men. That was the end of the problem. Ever since then, Ghom has welcomed tourists." Kathy made no attempt to hide the admiration in her voice. "Now Ghom has grown. It's entering the twentieth century, and all because of the Shahanshah." She half-turned in her seat and touched my arm. "He is a very great man."

"Are you hungry?" I asked.

"Starved."

"Is it safe to eat here?"

"It's all right to eat, but stay away from the water."

"Cholera?"

She shrugged. "There's always that danger. At the least, you're likely to get T.T."

" 'T.T.'?"

174

"Tehran Tummy: diarrhea. But there's a good restaurant around the corner. Great *chelo kabob*."

During lunch we spoke of other things while I wondered how Arsenjani was taking the news that I was missing. When we returned to the car I found that it had been washed, and I gave the man standing next to it with a wet rag enough *tomans* for a meal.

I invented a weak cover story about Nasser Razvan, Mehdi Zahedi and Firouz Maleki being acquaintances from the United States and had Kathy make a few more inquiries. That didn't take long in Ghom, and she turned up nothing. We headed back out into the desert. Now the heat was a physical presence beating down on the roof of the car, making the air in our lungs heavy and sodden.

The afternoon wore on. I turned a bend and saw the sun setting behind a gargantuan army truck that had tipped over on its side. Kathy was sleeping. I gently brought the car to a stop and got out to make sure the wreck was not recent, and that no one was injured. The cab was empty, and there was no way of determining how long the truck had been there; the desert air was dry as the sand, and I imagined that machinery could remain there for a long time without rusting.

A slight movement to my left attracted my attention, and I turned. There was a shack a few hundred yards away, almost obscured by a dune. In front of the shack a man was offering his praise to Allah; he was kneeling on a prayer rug, arms extended in front of him, his forehead touching the cooling sand. The dead, useless truck loomed in the foreground like a mummified dinosaur. I could not even imagine how the man sustained himself; he couldn't farm the sand, and there was no sign of any vehicle that could transport him to and from Ghom, Tehran or Esfahan. Still, he'd made it through one more day, and that was sufficient cause for him to offer praise and thanks to his God.

I walked slowly back to the car and found Kathy awake, brushing her hair.

"It's not far now," the girl said, her voice burnished by sleep. I got back behind the wheel and drove.

The outskirts of Esfahan, unlike those of Tehran, were meticulously clean and neat, the gray streets sprinkled with colorful shops. I'd had it for the day. "Are there any good hotels around here?"

"One of the finest in the world, but it's expensive."

"We can afford it." Considering my situation, I wasn't going to worry about money; I might wind up a very small overturned truck, but since Arsenjani had funded the trip in the first place, I was going to make sure I went out in style.

"The Shah Abbas is about five blocks straight ahead."

The Shah Abbas was everything Kathy had said it was, and more. Built on the site of an ancient caravansary—a meeting place of the caravans—the hotel displayed the kind of elegance that millions of dollars in government-supplied oil money can buy. And the elegance wasn't all facade; the staff was excellently trained, probably in Switzerland, and the service was impeccable. Unfortunately, I was in no mood to enjoy it; I was running low on adrenaline, gnarled taut with tension. I decided we'd fly the rest of the way.

In the morning, Kathy's face was beaming as she waited for me in the lobby.

"You look cheerful," I said. "Desert driving suits you."

"I feel like I'm finally starting to earn my keep," she said brightly. "You remember those names you asked me to look up? Well, I found one of them."

That woke me up. "What did you find out?"

"I got up early and checked through the Esfahan directory. There's a Nasser Razvan listed. I asked a few questions and it turns out that the Razvans are a well-known and very rich family. Their home's about half an hour's drive from the city."

The Nasser Razvan listed could well be the father. It figured: the young SAVAK agent from the well-to-do family. "Can you find out how to get there?"

"I already know. Do you think your friend will be there?"

"If he's not, I'll just say hello to the family."

"We'll need another car. I turned the other one in last night."

I motioned to the desk clerk.

The Razvan home could have been more accurately described as a plantation; it stretched for miles in all directions: acres of carefully tilled land filled with crops and fruit trees. I steered the car into the main drive and stopped in front of a massive wrought-iron gate. There was a cluster of servants' quarters behind and to the left of the gate. Farther up the drive, on the crest of a knoll, was the main compound, a Xanadu of multilevel dwellings all painted a glistening white. The front yard was a meadow boasting three Olympic-size pools of varying depths.

I pushed the buzzer on the gate. Instantly a man appeared at the door of one of the servants' houses and trotted to the gate. "I'm Dr. Frederickson," I said in Farsi. Kathy gave me a surprised sidelong glance. "This is Miss Martin. We're friends of the younger Nasser Razvan and have come to pay our respects to the family." The servant pondered this for a moment, then went back inside his house, presumably to telephone the main compound. I turned to Kathy. "From here on in, I'll do the talking."

Kathy nodded, her green eyes filled with questions. "You speak Farsi quite well."

"Just a few polite phrases," I said, avoiding her gaze.

The servant emerged once more and opened the gate. I

got back into the car and drove it slowly up the driveway, then parked in front of the largest of the houses at the top of the knoll. A man and woman on the far side of middle age came out the front door and walked toward us at a brisk pace, the woman a few steps behind her husband. Both had the robust good looks and sheen of health that, after a certain age, are usually by-products of money. Twenty years before, the woman had been ravishing; now she was handsome, dignified. The man had pure white hair, and I put his age at around sixty. His eyes were a clear blue, and he moved with an air of strength and character. I suspected he'd earned his money; a man doesn't develop the kind of metallic glint he had in his eyes by clipping coupons or sitting around watching oil flow through his backyard.

When I got out of the car, he offered me his hand. His grip was firm. "Our servant tells us you are friends of my son," the man said in heavily accented but intelligible English.

"Forgive us for imposing on you like this," I said, "but I was in a discussion involving your son and he certainly sounded like a man I'd like to meet. We were told he lived here, and I thought I'd drop in and say hello."

The man reached back and squeezed his beaming wife's hand. "Nasser is not here, but Shayesteh and I are very happy that you've come. You will, of course, stay for breakfast. My wife does not speak English, but if she could she would insist as I do."

"We can only stay for a few minutes."

"Nonsense! Allah would curse our home if we did not extend the hospitality of our household to admirers of our son. Come! We will eat!"

I took Kathy's arm and led her up the stone steps behind the man and his wife. I could feel the tension in her muscles; she knew I was lying, and I could only hope that she'd stick with me a few more minutes.

We entered a cavernous living room. A few moments later, as if by prearranged signal, a team of servants appeared bearing trays filled with tea, thick coffee, Iranian bread and pungent goat cheese.

The senior Razvan had festooned the walls of his home with photographs of his son, and Nasser Razvan, Jr.'s, presence was very real. In the pictures he was wearing a uniform; it made him look different, somehow older. I was sweating under the steady gaze of the man in the photographs. Fortunately, the elder Razvan didn't seem to mind carrying the burden of the conversation.

"I see your son is in the army," I said, pointing to one of the pictures.

Razvan made a modest gesture with his hand. "Nasser is the youngest major in the Iranian army."

And occupied an important post in the SAVAK, although that wasn't something the father was likely to discuss with a stranger. I complimented him on his land, and he grinned broadly. I waited while he translated the comment to his wife. Kathy was sitting as far away from me as she could get, in a corner. Her hands were clasped tightly together in her lap, and she was watching me closely.

"My landholdings took many years to build," Razvan said. "It was hard work, but it was also a pleasure, something that gave my life meaning. But now there is too much for just one man and his family. Large portions of my land have been broken up into parcels and given to the peasants by the Shah."

"That would be the 'White Revolution'?"

"Yes, and I am entirely for it. In fact, if I may say so, I was giving away land to my workers even before the Shah started his land-reform program."

It didn't surprise me; I instinctively liked the man and his wife. I wanted to ask about Mossadegh and the years of turmoil, but I couldn't think of a way of approaching the subject without arousing suspicion. I let the old man talk about his son, for that was obviously his favorite topic.

After fifteen minutes I rose to my feet. Kathy, with a sigh of relief, immediately stood. Razvan and his wife insisted that we stay longer, but I told him we had a plane to catch. The couple filled our hands with fruit, then escorted us to the door.

We hurried to the car, got in. Kathy's face was pale.

"What was your real reason for coming here, Dr. Frederickson?" she asked tensely. "You seemed very nervous. That lovely old couple didn't notice, but I did."

"I can't talk about it, Kathy," I said tightly. "The tour's over."

I'd been right on my first run-through at the beginning with Ali Azad: the photographs in the Razvan home had been of the young man others knew as Mehdi Zahedi. I now knew beyond doubt who Mehdi Zahedi was, *what* he was, and thought I had a pretty good idea why Arsenjani and the Shah had gone to such great lengths to try to convince me that Zahedi/Razvan was a big, bad terrorist: they'd been trying to use me to put one of their top agents back into place. The information was a death warrant, but—with a little luck—it just might be turned into a bargaining point: my total cooperation in exchange for Garth's safe return. And there was still the detailed report I'd sent to Phil Statler.

I drove slowly out the driveway, then stepped hard on the accelerator and headed toward the airport. "Listen to me, Kathy," I said quietly. "You must do exactly as I say. I find I have to cut my vacation short."

She turned away from me and stared out the window. We drove the rest of the way to the airport in silence. At the airport I pulled the car into a parking space and left the keys in the ignition. I hurriedly wrote out another three hundred dollars in traveler's checks and handed them to Kathy.

"I can't explain," I said, touching her hand. "You've been wonderful. Now you must take this money. Turn the car in, then fly back to Tehran. If anyone asks you about me, just tell them the truth: I hired you as my guide. Otherwise, don't say a word."

Tears welled in her eyes, making them look like circles of wet green plastic. *"Why*, Dr. Frederickson? What's this all about?"

"I just can't tell you any more. It's for your own safety, believe me."

"It has something to do with what happened back in that house, doesn't it?"

"Goodbye, Kathy." I grabbed my bag and headed into the terminal. I could feel the girl's eyes boring into my back.

14

As I'd suspected, much of what Arsenjani had told me about the deadly GEM and SAVAK maneuvering in New York was true; perfectly credible facts all designed to set me up for the whoppers he'd tried to lay on me. By February, the two-pronged battle in New York and Tehran must have been reaching a peak, and it had been a question of whether the Shah was going to get the GEM leaders before they got him. Firouz Maleki had been captured, and Mehdi Zahedi had been flown back on an emergency basis to interrogate the GEM operative. There was no question that Zahedi had intended to return quickly, because he hadn't even bothered to lay down a cover story to explain a longer absence.

Here things got cloudy: Something had happened to prevent Zahedi's return to the United States. Ali Azad had gotten nervous and hired John Simpson to investigate. Simpson, in an apparently miraculous wink of an investigative eye, had uncovered Orrin Bannon's operation, discovered Zahedi's real identity and role in the SAVAK, and tied it all together. Bannon had sent out an S.O.S., and Khordad had come running to try to protect Zahedi's cover. Simpson had been killed, but not before he'd shot up Khordad badly enough to prevent the Iranian strongman from running back to *his* cover.

Enter Phil Statler's ex-employee to raise enough suspicions to blow Zahedi out of the New York water. When all else had failed, they'd used Garth to get me to come to Iran.

I'd been feted, informed, lied to, flattered, the object of the game being to make me believe Zahedi was actually a GEM terrorist. I'd report this fact to Ali and eventually, as sure as the sun rises, Zahedi would pop up in New York to a rousing Confederation reception as the reincarnation of Che Guevara.

It could mean Garth was already dead, but—even assuming I could come up with a plan—I couldn't try to escape until I found out for sure. I'd have to confront Arsenjani and try to bargain for information about Garth and my way out of the country. But I was in no particular hurry now to see if the red in the carpet Arsenjani had rolled out for me was going to turn up blood. I'd turn myself over to the SAVAK in Shiraz. At the moment, I felt drawn to at least see Persepolis, the capstone of the culture that had brought Garth and me so much grief.

The plane took off five minutes after I boarded. I stared out the window as the plane ascended, banked, then headed toward Shiraz. The mountains and desert below were even more barren than the stretch between Tehran and Esfahan. We were heading south into a wasteland where the temperature often hit a hundred and forty degrees and the sand was drenched with oil. Beyond Shiraz were the shark-thick Persian Gulf and the tiny Arab Trucial States. It was a desolate landscape with its own brand of beauty and enormous wealth; it was a land a lot of people felt was worth dying for.

If I found out *Garth* was dead, I'd look for the first chance
—however slim—to take out the current head of the
SAVAK; the material and instructions I'd sent to Phil Statler
would knock out the New York SAVAK operation. I'd never
been fully optimistic about leaving Iran alive in the first
place.

The highway leading to Persepolis was new and wide, easy
driving. I studied the land around me for some portent of
what was to come, but there wasn't any; as a result, I was
totally unprepared for what I found rising into the sky at the
end of the highway.

Perhaps no Westerner could be prepared for the grandeur
of Persepolis. It was simply there, suddenly looming out of
the nothingness of the desert. In Italy, and across Europe,
conquerors had left ruins in their wake like great stone dung
droppings. Not in Iran. The rulers of the Persian Empire, a
civilization that had straddled most of the known world in
its time, had elected to draw together all of its grandeur in
one massive monument. What remained was in front of me.

After parking the car at the side of the road, I walked up a
long, sloping hillside to the acres of broken stone. I stopped
in front of a pillar with a cuneiform inscription, then turned
my attention to a large sign with an English translation that
had been erected beside it.

A great god is Ahuramazda; who created this Earth, who
created yonder heaven, who created man, who created wel-
fare for man, who made Xerxes king, one king of many, one
Lord of many. I am Xerxes the Great King, King of Kings,
King of the countries having every kind of people, King of
this great Earth far and wide, the son of Darius the King, an
Achaemenian. Says Xerxes the Great King: By the will of
Ahuramazda I made this colonnade for the representatives
of all countries; much else that is beautiful, I did in Persepo-

lis, and my father did. Whatever work seems beautiful, we did it all by the will of Ahuramazda. Says Xerxes the King: May Ahuramazda protect me and my kingdom: My work and my father's work. May Ahuramazda protect it!

No one could accuse Xerxes of modesty; but the author of those words had known what he was talking about. I'd read the words in English, but the surrounding ruins were the only translation needed; they rang in the hot, barren desolation of the Iranian desert like a broken bell whose echo would not die. In the stone stillness, Xerxes the King whispered in my ear.

Kathy had spoken at length about Persepolis, and I could almost imagine what the finished complex must have looked like: giant building blocks of stone hewn from Mount Rahmat, which loomed in the distance like some great, jealous god guarding its most prized possession; burnt brick, roof beams from Lebanon, floors of glazed tile and doors plated with precious metals; a vast wealth of gold, enamel, inlay work, matchless vases and statues. The treasure was gone, but fragments of the walls remained, and carved upon them were the histories of great battles, the struggle between Good and Evil. Mythical beasts and kings marched across the walls, all on a pilgrimage to this place, bearing tribute to the Shah, the mightiest of all.

Ahead and to my right, the Grand Staircase remained almost intact, a great highway of pitted stone leading up to a scarred, time-eroded platform that once had covered an area of 135,000 square meters. There was a small forest of stone columns, but the rest of the city had been broken into a vast field of unrecognizable shards—except for one startling sculpture: the upper half of a massive winged, two-headed bull lay on its side, staring with huge, unblinking, sightless eyes back across the centuries.

If there were other Iranian ruins comparable to Persepolis,

they were buried in the earth, and except for the new highway, a man came to the dead city on roads choked with dust and lined with the poor. Persepolis alone remained as a snatch of eternal poetry in the heart of a sad nursery rhyme. Now only the desert wind whistled through the shattered stone splinters of what had once been the Hall of a Hundred Columns. The underground water system ingeniously designed to catch and hold the rain was empty, leaving Persepolis as dry as the land bed on which it slept. But men still battled for the city's charms and the land to which they belonged.

The city had stood for two centuries before Alexander had come to sweep it away. They'd been fighting in Iran down through the ages, and it seemed I was a part of the latest war, in which Garth and Neptune had become casualties.

Standing in the midst of the ruins, I felt suddenly and profoundly *American*.

Persepolis, like a city of whispering stone, spoke to me of many things: I was a stranger in a totally alien culture, a very long way from home, lonely, homesick and very much afraid of dying without ever again seeing any face I loved.

I was certain that the city held other, less mystical, GEM secrets, but it was unlikely I'd ever learn them. I heard the footsteps behind me, but didn't bother to turn.

"It's too bad you didn't take my advice, dwarf. I rather like you." Arsenjani's voice was soft yet sharp, the tender thrust of a thin, finely honed knife. "Now I'm afraid I must ask you to come with me."

I turned and followed Arsenjani back to his car.

15

AT THE SHIRAZ POLICE STATION I was marched to a small room in the rear and motioned into a straight-backed chair. A bank of bright lights shone in my eyes, just like in the movies. The only other piece of furniture in the room was a desk with a scarred, warped top. Arsenjani settled down on that and we stared at each other. He didn't say anything; I didn't say anything. I was in no hurry; considering the fact that I had only one card, I didn't want to play my hand too soon.

I hadn't had anything to drink for a few hours, and my tongue felt twice its normal size. There were a glass and a carafe filled with water on the desk next to Arsenjani, and I assumed they were there as an incentive for me to give the right answers. That was assuming there were any questions left he didn't already know the answers to. He seemed in less of a hurry to ask questions than I was to get a drink, so I decided to try the direct approach.

"How about a glass of water for old times' sake?"

"Of course," Arsenjani said absently. He poured me a glass

from the carafe and I drank it down greedily. He refilled the glass and I drained it again; the water was cool and fresh. He offered me more, but I declined. My tongue was shrinking back to its normal size, and I didn't need a stomach cramp. Arsenjani covered the carafe and pushed it behind him. "It seems you've discovered our little secret," he continued drily. He was still smiling, but his eyes were colder than it ever gets in Iran.

"What have you done with the girl? She doesn't know anything."

"We're aware of that. She's already been in touch with us."

That came like a blow in the stomach. I thought of the young girl with the wheat-colored hair and green eyes and felt a sense of betrayal I knew I had no right to feel.

"Naturally, we'd been looking for you," Arsenjani continued. "Her call saved us—and her—a lot of trouble. Her behavior may shock you but, you see, Miss Martin knows Iran; when in doubt, call the police. She was simply protecting herself."

Given enough time to think about it, I'd probably decide she'd done the right thing. In any case, I had other things to worry about at the moment. The door opened and I glanced up at the man who entered. He wore a military uniform. The major's insignia on the collar tabs harmonized with his commanding presence and clashed with his youth. I didn't need an introduction.

Mehdi Zahedi/Nasser Razvan looked even more undernourished than his pictures—a condition even the tailored uniform couldn't quite compensate for. His skin looked like brown crayon over chalk; it was the kind of pallor a man gets from spending a lot of time in a hospital.

Zahedi was no Atlas, but then he didn't need to be. His eyes were a hot, wet black, and he moved with an electric air of complete confidence and authority that made him seem about a foot taller and fifty pounds heavier than he was. I was sorry I'd never heard him speak; I imagined he could really set a crowd to humming.

"Greetings from the Confederation of Iranian Students." I'd intended to sound ironic, but it came out merely silly.

"Dr. Frederickson," Zahedi said, bowing slightly. He spoke with a New Yorker's accent, and I found that amusing; it was so amusing it made me even more homesick. "I've heard a lot about you, and I've seen you on campus many times. You're called Mongo by your friends."

"A lot of your ex-friends are going to be calling *you* 'spy.'"

"*You* call me a spy. Ali and the others call me a revolutionary."

"Not anymore. Things change."

"Some things change, but this isn't one of them. I'll be returning to New York soon, but that isn't your concern."

"My brother is my concern. There's no more need to bullshit. Did you kill him?"

"We'll ask the questions," Arsenjani snapped.

"Look," I said, deciding it was as good a time as any to slap my one card down hard on the table, "I've still got something to offer you. You're hot to get Boy Wonder here back into place in New York. Frankly, I don't give a shit what you Persians do to each other, so I'll cooperate with you. I can easily give Ali such a story as you would not believe. *If* you release Garth, I'll help you provide a cover for your man."

Arsenjani made a clucking sound. "I'm not sure we can trust you."

"I'll write him a report, tell him I'm planning to stay on in Iran for a couple of months. At the rate things have been heating up, in two or three months either you'll have crushed GEM or you'll all be fighting in the trenches. My only price is that you let Garth go." My next words were forced out of me as I felt tears well in my eyes and I desperately fought them back. "For Christ's sake, at least *tell* me if he's dead."

"We have our own excellent forgers," Arsenjani said. "A report along the lines you propose is already being prepared."

"All right, you pricks," I said heatedly. "I'll tell you what's going to happen if we can't get down to some serious negotiations. Before I left I sent a detailed report to . . . someone. That someone will open it and release the information to my press contacts if he doesn't hear from me *soon*. Those contacts will *dig*, and you'll *really* be screwed when the newspapers get hold of this story. Old Himself, assuming he stays alive much longer, will be *very* unhappy with you. You'd at least better check with him before you do something stupid."

Arsenjani smiled thinly, then leaned over to the other side of the desk and pulled a drawer open. He drew out a large envelope and dropped it on the desk. I could feel the blood rush from my heart, and for a moment I felt faint. It was the report I'd sent to Phil Statler. My card had turned up a joker.

"Those fuckers at Military Intelligence put a mail cover on Statler and me," I whispered, suddenly short of breath.

"I'm afraid so," Zahedi said softly, moving closer to me. "Now that we've gotten that out of the way, perhaps we *can* talk seriously. Colonel Arsenjani thinks you may know more than you think you do—or are telling us. You'd be well advised to cooperate."

"I'm all cooperated out," I said, feeling drained but trying to gather enough strength for a quick killing attack on one of them. "I know what you're after, but I can't help you. I haven't got the slightest idea who the GEM leader is. That isn't what I was being paid to find out."

Zahedi scratched his head, grunted. "I wonder. There may be somebody you contacted, or who contacted you, who at least made you suspicious. Think about it."

"I have thought about it. I have no ideas, not even an opinion. Look, Mehdi, or Nasser, or whatever your name is—"

"Mehdi is fine. Actually, I'm rather used to it."

"All right, Mehdi, here I am chatting with the cream of the SAVAK. If you couldn't find the GEM leaders in all the time *you've* been working on it, what makes you think I could have done it in a few weeks?"

"There are other questions we're interested in," Zahedi said, eyeing me intently.

"Me too. Why didn't you turn right around and fly back to New York after Firouz Maleki died? You must have known Ali would get hyper."

"I said *we* will ask all questions," Arsenjani repeated softly, menacingly. "So far you are not doing well, Frederickson."

"Tough shit," I said to Arsenjani. And to Zahedi: "You put on a great act for Ali and his boys, but now it's over. Your cover was broken when John Simpson found out who you really are. It's still broken, and all the king's camels aren't going to put it together again. You left tracks: Simpson found them, I found them, and in the fuutre somebody else is going to find them. Your career in the United States is over." I paused, shot a glance at Arsenjani, who was quietly tracing patterns on the desk top with his finger, looked back at Zahedi. "By the way, how *did* Simpson find out you're Nasser Razvan? And how did he make the connection so quickly between you and Orrin Bannon?"

"*Now* we are getting to the crux of the matter," Zahedi said sharply, pointing a long, bony index finger at my forehead.

I didn't know, but it was a question to which I'd been giving a lot of thought. Zahedi was too experienced and good to leave chicken tracks behind, even if he was in a hurry; yet John Simpson had gathered enough information in just a few days to get himself killed. I didn't believe it was imply good detective work; there hadn't been time. And it hadn't been luck. Luck is one thing, walking on water something else again.

"Obviously, somebody tipped him off," I said. "There's no other way he could have tracked Zahedi so quickly."

"Of *course*," Arsenjani interjected impatiently. "But *who* gave him the information?"

"Probably somebody in the SAVAK, Arsenjani. That's a ho-ho-ho on you boys."

"*Who?*" Arsenjani snapped.

"Hey, c'mon! How the hell do you expect me to know? *I* wasn't the one who got tipped."

"You weren't shown a list of SAVAK agents in the United States?"

"No," I said, puzzled.

The question also seemed to take Zahedi by surprise. He turned to Arsenjani and spoke in Farsi, too rapidly for me to follow. But I was certain he was asking his superior about the list. Arsenjani shook his head impatiently.

"I love it," I said, grinning. "You mean there may be a list of SAVAK agents floating around somewhere in the United States?"

"Never mind," Arsenjani snapped. "If you weren't shown such a list, then how did *you* find out so much?"

"Riding a dead man's coattails, and a little luck. I read Simpson's notes and made a few guesses." Arsenjani made a noise in his throat which I didn't like; it sounded as though he were getting ready to spit me out. "C'mon, Zahedi," I said quickly, "why didn't you go back to the United States when you had the chance?"

"Cholera," Zahedi said after a long pause, ignoring a sharp glance from his boss. "I was exposed. Naturally, I had the best medical care, but by the time the disease had run its course the damage had already been done."

"Ali Azad had already hired Simpson, and somebody had put Simpson on your trail."

"Yes," Zahedi said easily. "The rest is history."

It seemed half a lifetime since Phil Statler had come to me with his problem of a missing muscle act. I was very tired. I slumped in my chair and tried to look defeated, which wasn't very difficult. I'd given up hope of ever finding out what had happened to Garth, and I was looking for an opening to get at one of my interrogators. "It's just a damn shame the bright young star of the SAVAK can't play spy at the university anymore," I said softly to Zahedi, playing for time.

"Well, as I said, I think your concern is premature," Zahedi said pleasantly. "I enjoy working in your country."

The pale young man lighted a cigarette, coughed, then absently reached behind his boss for the carafe of water. Arsenjani grasped the younger man's wrist and shook his head. It was a small gesture, almost imperceptible, but it bothered me enough to make the sweat on my body turn cold. Circuits were trying to close somewhere in the back of my mind. "If Garth and I don't go back, there are going to be some nasty questions raised."

"Really?" Arsenjani said mockingly. "And who will raise these questions?"

"Phil Statler, for one. Garth and I have a lot of friends. Sooner or later someone is going to dig up this whole mess. And Ali's not stupid. There isn't going to be any rousing welcome for Mehdi if *I* turn up missing, report or no report. You'd better hope Garth and I die of old age, because that's the *only* thing anyone's going to believe. Your American operation is blown no matter what you do. Since it won't serve any purpose to kill us, you might as well let us go."

"You can't be serious," Zahedi said.

I laughed nervously. "I thought I had a pretty good argument."

"You've imperiled a carefully planned operation," Arsenjani said, real anger shimmering in his voice. "And nothing less than the security of our nation and the life of the Shahanshah is at stake!"

"Imperiled, shit," I said with a kind of desperate fury. "It's *ruined*. Can't you see that's the point? This business was your game, not mine. You gambled and you lost; let it go now. Besides, you've given fair warning to even the dumbest revolutionaries that you're breathing down their necks."

Zahedi was looking down, studying the toe of his polished jackboot, which he was tapping up and down. Arsenjani stared at me a long time; his dark eyes looked as if they'd been flash-frozen in his head. Finally he shifted his gaze to Zahedi and snapped his fingers. Two guards who'd been waiting outside the door marched in.

"Take him out," Arsenjani said softly.

The presence of the guards surprised me, and I knew I'd waited too long. Still, I thought I might have a shot at Zahedi. I lunged out of the chair at him, but he was quicker— or I was slower—than I'd anticipated; he quickly stepped to one side and hit me on the side of the head. By then the guards were on me. I caught the first one with a stiff jab to the solar plexus. The second guard grabbed me around the neck. I twisted, bringing my knee up hard against the inside of his knee. That set him down. I crouched and spun, but it was too late; Arsenjani was on me like a cat. He parried one blow and brought the butt of his gun down on the top of my head. There was a sound like corn popping inside my skull. I listened to it for a while, then drifted off to sleep.

16

I CAME OUT OF IT to find myself tied and lying in the back of an army truck. My head felt twice its normal size, but there didn't seem to be any permanent damage from Arsenjani's expertly placed blow. The skin might be broken, but not much; Arsenjani had sapped me with loving care. That meant an accident of some sort was the next order of the day.

The truck bumped along, and sand drifted in through the slats on the side: desert. But I had other things to think about. Something was going on inside my body that I didn't understand. My head seemed to be growing larger instead of smaller, and this sensation of swelling was crawling down through my neck to my chest and stomach. My lungs felt as if somebody were scraping steel wool across them. Alternately burning and freezing, my body seemed to be floating above the boards, and my clothes were soaked with sweat. Some giant was squeezing me like a sponge. I smelled of fever.

Then, without warning, everything inside me came loose;

my stomach churned and I vomited, splattering a thick stream of yellow bile on myself and the rough floorboards of the truck. I rolled away from it and only succeeded in soiling the other side. The air inside the truck was suddenly thick with the fetid smell of disease and human waste.

It wouldn't stop gushing, and with my hands tied behind my back, I was in trouble—literally in danger of drowning in my own vomit. I'd completely lost control of my body functions; at the rate I was losing fluids, I knew it wouldn't take long to die.

Not that I particularly cared at the moment; dying seemed a perfectly reasonable means of escape from the smell and the agony. Still . . . death is a long time, and old habits are hard to break. I struggled up to my knees and braced myself against the lurching slats until the spasms finally passed. Then I aimed for a relatively dry area of the truck bed and passed out.

I woke up when the truck braked to a stop. The only sound I could hear was a high-pitched buzzing in my ears; now my head felt like a huge balloon filled with rotten air. My vision was blurred, but there was a relatively clear central core, like the distant end of a tunnel. I watched down its length as a soldier opened the rear door. He didn't like what he saw and smelled: he froze, his eyes wide with terror, then retched. A second soldier appeared, turned and started to run.

"Halt!" a deep voice boomed in Farsi. The command was punctuated with a pistol shot that sounded to me like somebody spitting. An officer I hadn't seen before moved into the end of the tunnel. He was wearing rubber gloves and a gauze mask that covered his nose and mouth. The two soldiers returned meekly, prodded by the baleful eye of the officer's gun. The officer produced two more sets of gloves and masks, which the men put on.

"Get him out," the officer commanded.

It was all surreal: the terrified eyes above the masks, the gloved hands pawing at my soiled and stinking body. The two men pulled me out of the truck and let me fall to the ground. My lungs felt like dirty rags, trying and failing to suck in enough air to feed my oxygen-starved body. The ringing in my ears grew louder. Something very dark and evil was growling in a corner of my mind, but it was impossible to hold a single thought for more than a moment and I couldn't yet see what it was.

The officer opened the cab of the truck, removed a knapsack and water bag and threw them down beside me. The water bag meant something to me, but I wasn't sure exactly what. It could mean an end to the torture of my thirst, but my hands and feet were still tied. I opened my mouth to beg, but no sounds came out. The officer produced a field knife, stepped behind me and cut my ropes. Then the three men got back into the truck and drove away.

I rolled my eyes and could see only sand. Finally my gaze fastened on the water bag. Suddenly, in my fevered mind, the water bag became a carafe on a desk in a police station. I remembered Arsenjani offering me a glass of water, watching me drink, then refusing Zahedi the same courtesy. And I knew.

Cholera. Tainted water. Arsenjani, my smooth, thoughtful host, had given me cholera-infected water to drink. *That* had been his solution to the problem posed by a certain dwarf; the Iranian Government certainly could not be held responsible if I wound up with a case of cholera and died in the desert. After all, it was common knowledge that the cholera vaccine was only forty percent effective, no protection at all in the event of direct exposure. If they'd arranged something as neat for Garth, Ali just might buy the "report" he received from me attesting to Zahedi's revolutionary activities.

Rage stiffened my muscles and brought me to my feet. I staggered around in a circle, but finally managed to reach the water bag. It occurred to me that this water also might be contaminated, but I doubted it; the damage had already been done. It wouldn't have made any difference to me anyway; my thirst was overwhelming.

I opened the top of the bag and poured a few quarts over my face; some of it made its way down my throat, and that cleared my head a little. I stumbled a few steps and sat down hard on the packed sand. I heaved the bag over my shoulder and drank some more, then promptly vomited again. I might be able to put water into my body, but there was no way I could manage to keep it there.

The thought of dying of cholera in the desert like an animal should have terrified me, but it didn't. I tried to care and couldn't. The cholera was striking with terrible, numbing swiftness.

I tried to remember what I'd read of the disease: At the moment, germs transmitted by the contaminated water were making a shambles of the normal flora in my intestinal tract, turning the usually benign assemblage against its host. In the final stages the bacteria would be eating away chunks of my stomach and intestines—literally consuming my body. In the end, cholera killed by dehydrating the body. I was a dead man: treatment had to be immediate, and the chance of that looked rather slim from where I was sitting in the middle of the desert. I was about to become a statistic, a spent human bullet fired by the SAVAK.

My body voided itself once again, and the reaction left a dull ache in my belly that worked its way up into my chest cavity and down into my legs. My vision now consisted of tiny bright pinpricks of light that burned flickering images on my fever-hot brain. I closed my eyes against the pain, then put my hands on the sand and shoved. Up on my feet, I leaned forward, trying to walk, then realized that I wasn't walking at all, but only imagining it. I emptied the water bag and pressed my face into the wet sand.

Then I began experiencing other hallucinations; I imagined I could hear the sound of an approaching jeep grinding through its gears as it wallowed through the sand. It struck me that Arsenjani was impatient, already sending his men back to see if I was dead.

Rubbery hands grabbed for me, and I opened my eyes to find myself looking up into more masked faces, I struck out at the blurred images, grabbed for one of the masks, missed and sank down into an oblivion that smelled like the bowels of hell, and was me.

17

I DREAMED. White-robed figures were bending over me, cleaning me when I soiled myself, sticking needles into my arms and legs, inserting tubes into my nose and throat. Between these recurring dreams was darkness, like a shutter banging up and down.

Gradually the smell of my own body decreased and the rubber sack that was my head began to deflate. Finally the clear fever dreams merged into blurred reality. It occurred to me that I wasn't dead yet, and that the needles in my arms and legs were real, as were the man and woman who took turns standing over me. In the beginning their faces were covered with the familiar gauze masks. Then, after a particularly long, dreamless sleep, I awoke to find the masks gone. They were both at the side of my bed, smiling down at me. The room smelled of flowers.

"You're going to be all right, Mongo," the man said cheerfully.

I tried to reply, but the muscles in my mouth and throat felt rigid, like stiff plastic. I managed to lift one hand, then

200

went back to sleep. When I awoke again, I felt stronger. I sat up and would have spoken if there'd been anybody to talk to. The room was empty.

There were a vase of flowers and a huge basket of fruit on a night table next to my bed. My mouth watered; it felt as if I hadn't eaten anything in about ten years. I selected a large apple from the basket and bit into it; the juices from the apple squirted against the inside of my mouth, puckering the soft, sore flesh. I chewed slowly, savoring the exquisite taste of the fruit, then closed my eyes. When I opened them again, a man was standing in the doorway.

This one I knew. It was Darius: Khayyam, not the King. I wondered why I felt so little surprise at seeing him there; perhaps it was because I knew it all finally came down to a simple process of elimination. There couldn't be many men with the personal stature to organize and lead an insurrection, to form and lead an organization like GEM. Darius Khayyam filled the bill.

He strode quickly across the room and gripped my shoulder. "Mongo, my friend. Welcome back to the world of the living."

I put the apple down on the table and looked up into his eyes. They seemed harder, colder than I remembered. Or maybe I'd never really looked into them before.

"So *you're* the mastermind they're trying to dig out of the woodwork. Son-of-a-bitch!"

Darius' smile was wan, bittersweet. "Yes," he said distantly, "but I'm afraid that phase of the operation is over. They were close; very close." His eyes came back into focus and he pressed the tips of his fingers together. "Now the game will get rougher. I hope our organization is up to it."

He pulled a chair up to the side of the bed, and I touched his arm. "Darius, do you know anything about my brother?"

His eyes clouded. "SAVAK," he said softly.

"But is he *alive*?"

"I'm sorry, Mongo. I don't know."

"He *could* be alive?"

"It's possible. I wouldn't get my hopes up. Is there anything I can get you?"

"I'm hungry as hell," I said. And I *would* keep my hopes up.

"Food will be brought in a few minutes." There was an embarrassed silence during whch both of us avoided each other's eyes. Now, at what seemed the end, there didn't appear to be much left to say. "I'm sorry you had to go through this torment, Mongo," Darius said into the silence. "I did try to warn you."

"You saved my life, probably at considerable risk to your own."

Darius shrugged wearily. As usual, he was wearing a conservatively cut business suit, and looked as if he might have stopped off to see me on his way to the university; except that he'd been spending a lot of time lately in that one suit. It was soiled and baggy, like the puffy flesh under his tired eyes.

"How long has it been since you slept?" I asked.

"It doesn't matter."

"How did you know where I was?"

I wasn't sure he was going to answer, but he finally said, "We have our own sources of information. We knew you'd be picked up after you visited the Razvan home. Our fear was that they'd execute you outright, or throw you in prison. Then we wouldn't have been able to help."

"I was pretty sure I was going to be one dead dwarf."

"Cholera can be treated if it's caught in time. We were able to keep replenishing your body fluids until the disease had run its course. *Finding* you was more difficult; we followed the truck into the desert. Naturally, we had to keep a good distance between us, and it took more than an hour to locate you after they'd dumped you."

I tried to think of something profound to say; it came out "Thank you."

Darius cleared his throat. "Our motives aren't entirely altruistic, Mongo. You're my friend, but that's not the reason you're alive. *Many* of my friends, not to mention my sister, have died in the past few years. Many more are now rotting in prison. In other words, the fact that you are my friend would not in itself be a reason for me to risk my life and the lives of those who have sheltered and cared for you."

"I'm an investment, then?"

He thought about it, nodded. "Yes, an investment: a witness to the ruthlessness of this regime, and insurance that Mehdi Zahedi won't be going back to the United States."

This particular bullet had been picked up from the desert sand, brushed off, and was about to be fired by the other side. I was beginning to feel slightly used. "You're *here* now. What difference does it make where Zahedi is? I'd think you'd *want* him back in the United States so he'd be out of your hair here."

Darius shook his head. "There are others in New York who must continue to operate in secrecy. Also, the time for open fighting has not yet arrived. I've prepared carefully. No one else at the university will question my absence; they think I'm on a sabbatical. Zahedi would know immediately what happened, and I can't have that. There would be too much pressure on us here."

"You're assuming that I'll cover for you."

"Yes, I am," Darius said, a faint note of surprise in his voice. "Am I wrong?"

"I won't betray you, and you know it. But *you're* the one who canceled friendship out of this particular equation. The only reason I'm alive is that you want something from me."

"It's true I said that. I have a great responsibility; I wanted to make you understand."

"I appreciate your honesty, and I understand."

The air cleared, Darius smiled and handed me another apple. I finished that and had an orange as a chaser. Darius produced a pack of American cigarettes. I lighted one, but it tasted terrible and I ground it out. "Where are we?" I asked.

"In the home of friends."

"I'd like to thank them."

"They have their thanks."

The wariness in Darius' voice served to remind me that I could be captured again, and he didn't want me to know any more than I had to. I changed the subject. "How long have I been here?"

"A week. Much of the time you've been under sedation; it speeds the recuperative process."

"What happens now?"

He gently touched my arm. "I realize you're still very weak, my friend, but we must leave."

It made sense. Every moment I stayed there meant danger for everyone involved. By now Arsenjani and Zahedi would be having fits at not being able to find my corpse, and they weren't likely to believe I'd ascended bodily into heaven. That would mean a house-to-house search of the area. "Where will we go?"

"There are places." The wariness again.

"But you won't tell me where?"

"Eventually. For now it's better if you simply follow instructions. You're still not out of the country."

"They have my passport."

"All will be taken care of."

"Darius, I can't leave until I find out what's happened to Garth."

"If your brother is alive, I promise you GEM will do what it can to get him safely out of Iran. There's absolutely nothing you can do on your own—except get yourself, and me, killed."

He was right. As much as it rankled, it was time for me to go home.

Food was brought by a maid who carefully avoided looking at either of us. I ate quickly. Despite my hunger, the food tasted flat; it seemed it was going to take my taste buds longer than my appetite to fully recover. I downed three cups of steaming tea, then got out of bed. I was a little wobbly, but I managed to dress in the clothes someone had laid out for me on a chair. They were hand-sewn and fitted fairly well. Darius watched me in silence. I knew I wasn't going to get any more from him than he wanted to tell me, but I decided to test the limits.

"Did you have this whole GEM thing planned before you left Iran?"

"No," Darius said after a moment's hesitation. "As I told you back in New York, I was not a political man at that time. I left finally because everything around me reminded me too much of my sister. Call it guilt at my own noninvolvement. It never occurred to me that the government responsible for killing her should—much less *could*—be replaced. That came much later."

"What changed your mind?"

Darius inclined his head to the left and touched his forehead in a distinctive and peculiar gesture I'd seen many times before. Finally he smiled. "*Irreverence*," he said at last, smoothing his long white hair back into place. "Specifically, the irreverence I found in the United States. It's good that men should be irreverent; it keeps them from taking themselves and the things they do too seriously. Irreverence is the perfect antidote to the poison of kings."

"And you're the most irreverent of all; the top man."

"That isn't quite the way I'd put it."

"How would you put it?"

"It's true that I put GEM together, but now there are a

number of 'top men.' I'm principally a theorist and organizer."

"If you knew how hard they're working to nail you, you wouldn't be so modest."

"Over the past few years many men have risked and sacrificed their lives while I've lived comfortably in the United States."

"How did you maintain secrecy? Men don't lie well when they're being tortured."

"A man can't tell what he doesn't know. We used a pyramidal command structure composed of triangular personnel modules. I'll discuss it with you one day in what I hope will be happier times."

"I'm familiar with the structure; they used it in Algiers."

"It's a good system, but not perfect. Key personnel were being captured, and when that happens the central pyramid begins to crumble. Zahedi was very close to the truth. That's why I'm here."

"Pyramid," I said. "You've been living in the United States. There has to be somebody else at your level here in Iran, a top operational chief who makes sure that your plans are carried out. Also, you're wired into the SAVAK, right?"

Darius remained silent, and I knew I'd reached the limit. That was one more thing I'd have to ask Darius in happier times. I'd like to meet the man who'd spent all this time operating under the SAVAK's nose; he had to be a genius.

Darius led me out of the house through a back door and motioned me into a waiting pickup truck. The bed of the truck was covered with a canvas tarpaulin. "I'll have to ask you to get in the back," Darius said. "I'm afraid you'd be easily recognized."

"I can't imagine why," I said, crawling under the tarpaulin.

That much exercise promptly put me to sleep. I zipped through three or four recurring nightmares and woke up when somebody yanked back the tarpaulin. That levitated me about two feet into the air, but it was only Darius.

"We're here, Mongo. How do you feel?"

"You just scared the hell out of me and I ache all over, in that order."

"I'm sorry there isn't more time to rest."

"You worry about my transportation and I'll worry about my beauty sleep."

"Agreed."

"If you don't mind, I'd like to be dropped off at Times Square."

"Ah. Regrettably, your tour ends at Kennedy Airport. After that you'll have to fend for yourself."

"That'll do, assuming there isn't a cab strike."

"You're also responsible for getting yourself out of the truck."

"Don't you want to blindfold me?"

"That won't be necessary."

I climbed out. The truck with its silent driver pulled away, and I glanced around me. We were back at Persepolis, on the slope of the mountain overlooking the ruins. Darius immediately started off up a rocky trail leading along the base of a cliff. I followed, but lost him twenty minutes later when he turned a corner.

Feeling very foolish, I stood on the spot in the trail where Darius had disappeared. My repertoire of magic incantations being rather limited, I waited. A moment later Darius appeared from behind a large outcropping of rock at the side of the trail. He pulled the "rock" to one side and I could see that it was a painted, dirt-encrusted canvas sheet covering the entrance to a cave.

"You're the first American to see this," Darius said. "In fact, this particular entrance has eluded even the Iranian archaeologists."

Stepping into the gloom, I felt a damp chill. Darius lifted a torch from a bracket on the wall and dipped it into a vat of oil at the side of the entrance; he touched a match to the wide end and the torch burst into flame.

"Not as convenient as battery lamps," he said, "but more dependable."

The light penetrated only a few feet into the darkness, but that was enough for me to see that the small cave branched off into three tunnels. "Where are we?"

"The Persian catacombs," he said. "It's part of the original aqueduct system built for Persepolis. The conduits stretch for miles under the mountains. Stay close behind me; if you get lost, it could be centuries before anyone found you."

I followed Darius into the middle tunnel, moving along paths that had been worn by slaves and artisans thousands of years in the past. The man-made tunnels intersected with other, natural tunnels that even a tall man like Darius could comfortably walk in. I wondered how many millions of man-hours had gone into the construction of the system.

"The government may not know about that particular entrance," I said, "but they certainly know about the aqueduct system. It must have occurred to the SAVAK that you could be hiding guns and supplies here; it occurred to *me*. You must bring them in across the Gulf, probably through Iraq."

He shrugged noncommittally. "I'm sure it's occurred to them, but the system is so vast that it would be next to impossible to find something unless you knew exactly where to look."

We emerged from the tunnel into a large room carved from the rock by some prehistoric underground river. Here the light was supplied by bulbs strung across the ceiling and powered by a gasoline generator; all the conveniences of modern living.

The crates of precious LS-180s were stacked up along the opposite wall and clashed with the ancient, stony decor surrounding them. "Your arsenal," I said. "Enough for a good many forays, but not enough to sustain any kind of prolonged guerrilla operation."

Darius smiled. "But this is only a small fraction of our arms, smuggled into the country piece by piece over the years. They're not all LS-180s, to be sure; we've only been able to obtain them in the past year. The rest is hidden in various caches around the country." He glanced at his watch. "You'll be safe here until it's time for you to travel, which will be in a few hours."

"How will you get my brother away from the SAVAK, assuming he's still alive?"

He looked at me reprovingly. "I haven't promised anything, Mongo. You must be content with the belief that we'll do whatever is possible without unduly jeopardizing the lives of our own people."

"Okay. How do you plan to get me out of the country without a passport?"

He smiled wryly. "By the same route the guns come in— and you've already guessed that. At ten, a guide will meet you in the desert two miles due west of here. You'll be taken to the Gulf, across that into Kuwait, then north into Iraq. You'll receive further instructions at that time. Have you ever ridden a camel?"

"You've got to be kidding; I can barely handle a bicycle."

Darius laughed. For a moment he reminded me of the gentle professor I'd known at the university. "Nonsense: I'm aware of your athletic abilities. You should have a *wonderful* time; it will be an experience you'll never forget."

"Goddamn it, Darius, I'm *serious*."

"So am I," he said, still laughing. "The camel is an unjustly slandered beast. You'll have no trouble as long as the one you're riding *takes* to you."

"Yeah? How can I tell if he's going to take to me?"

"If a camel likes you, he won't bite."

"Jesus *Christ!*"

Darius turned serious again. "The journey to the Gulf should take you about two days; you'll ride only at night. Once you're in Iraq, you'll be safe. As I've indicated, arrangements have already been made for a passport and transportation back to the United States."

There was something about the whole business that still wasn't quite right. It was rattling around in my brain like a pebble in a shoe, but I couldn't put my finger on it.

"You must eat and sleep again, if you can," Darius continued. "There'll be little opportunity for either when you're out on the desert."

Darius produced a small Sterno unit and heated some rice, which we ate in silence. After that I lay down on a pile of rugs in a corner. I didn't think I could sleep any more, which was an indication of how little I knew about the wasting effects of cholera.

This time I dreamed of men and land and power, and of dead men who had dreamed the same dreams. I dreamed of a planet covered with people, a shrinking orb where there were no new worlds to conquer—only the old ones left for men to do battle and die for, a deadly game of musical chairs played with ideology and real estate.

Despite the dreams, I awoke refreshed. Darius handed me a small sack and a canteen of water; inside the sack were a compass and a few handfuls of nuts and dried fruit.

"It's time," Darius said.

More torches and tunnels. This time the way was more tortuous, and it slanted upward. Finally Darius extinguished the torch and we crawled the last fifty yards on our bellies with a hot desert wind blowing in our faces. At the end was a crypt, and beyond that a huge platform cut into the sharply sloping side of the mountain. Aside from the narrow hole we'd squeezed through to reach the crypt, there were no secrets here; the platform was littered with candy wrappers, soda bottles and a stray prophylactic or two: the ubiquitous footprints of the tourist. A hundred feet below the lip of the platform, the ruins stretched across the landscape like scattered bones bleached by the bright moonlight.

"Remember this place when you return home, my friend," Darius said, pointing to the dead city. "The Persians ruled a great empire for thousands of years. Once we were an enlightened people, one of the greatest civilizations the world has ever known. But the time of kings is past. One day, if it is Allah's will, we will learn to use our riches wisely. With the proper leadership, we'll be great again."

Now it was Darius who listened to the whispering of the ruins; he stood for more than a minute in complete silence staring out at them. Then he abruptly turned and pointed above and to the left where a faint trail cut a scar up and across the face of the mountain. "Follow the path to the other side," he continued matter-of-factly. "Then remember to walk due west. Your guide will be waiting for you."

"How do I get up to the trail?"

"You'll have to climb." He pointed toward the lip of the platform. "Most of the way is easy going, but the first thirty or forty yards are fairly steep. Be careful."

"What about you?"

"I have work to do."

"Try not to get yourself killed, okay?"

"Goodbye, my friend."

"Goodbye, hell. After you take over this quaint little desert community, I expect to be named an honorary citizen."

"You've earned it."

"*And* Grand Exalted Vizier."

"Yes. That will be fine. We'll create the post specially for you."

"You . . . won't forget about Garth."

"I won't forget."

I was reaching for his hand when the searchlight came on above me; the light hit me full in the face, piercing my eyes like hot wires. I reacted instinctively, throwing my arms up over my face and staggering to the edge of the circle of light.

"Don't move!" The command came in English. It was Arsenjani's voice.

Darius lunged forward and pushed me out of the light. That didn't do much good; where we were standing there were vertical walls of rock on either side of the platform. I tripped and fell—an opportune pratfall that saved my life; there was the sharp report of a rifle and the rock above my head sprouted obscene little splinters of death. Once again the searchlight found me and held. There was the sound of feet clambering down the mountainside above us.

Darius stepped back, spun around and stuck his hand inside his shirt. The spotlight swung back, gripping him. His hand came out empty, but his body began to twitch under the incessant prompting of automatic-weapons fire; he danced like a crippled puppet as the slugs tore through his body. His silver hair turned to a crown of blood.

Darius had never had a gun; he'd reached inside his shirt knowing that the move would cost him his life, hoping that the soldiers' attention would be momentarily distracted from me. Now I had to find a way to take advantage of his sacrifice. I sprang to my feet and ran low against the barrier of the wall. The light swung back and forth, searching for me while bullets splattered against the rock face where I'd been standing only moments before. It was one of the few times in my life I've been happy to be a dwarf: there are a vast host of disadvantages, but being an easy target isn't one of them.

There didn't seem to be anything beyond the lip of the platform but empty space, but there was no other place to go. Besides, I preferred killing myself on the rocks below to giving Arsenjani the satisfaction of having his men load me up with lead. I rolled the last few feet and dropped over the edge of the platform. Finding myself bouncing down a steep incline, I dug my feet and fingers into some soft shale, breaking my fall. The light swung out and evaporated in the darkness over my head.

There was chaos on the platform. Men were running across the stone, firing at the shadows and one another until Arsenjani gave the order to stop. He spoke in Farsi. "He has to be somewhere in the rocks! Find him!"

Finding me wasn't going to be particularly difficult; a matter of a few minutes, at most. Even if I could somehow make it to the ruins below, I'd only be a moving target in the moonlight; small as I was, they had to get me eventually.

The side of the mountain above me was now covered with soldiers converging on the sound of the gunfire, blocking the only route to the desert. Somehow, Arsenjani had known we would be somewhere on or in the mountain, and the sound of our voices had given us away. *How* he'd known where we'd be was another question I wasn't likely ever to learn the answer to.

But if I had to die, I still wanted to take Zahedi or Arsenjani with me. Killing Mehdi Zahedi would be a distinct pleasure, but Arsenjani was my odds-on favorite candidate; it was the SAVAK chief who'd given me infected water to drink, then left me alone in the desert to sweat, vomit and defecate my guts out. But in the end I'd take whichever man gave me the better opportunity.

I inched my way across the mountainside, past the vertical line of the wall rising from the platform. A knot of soldiers on the lip of the platform to my left were shining powerful flashlights down into the gloom below. One of them carried a heavy climbing rope, which explained how they'd made it down to the ledge so quickly. I pressed back into the shadow of the rocks and remained there until the soldiers moved on to another position. I could just make out some of their conversation.

"He must have fallen."

"Spread out across the top of the mountain; He may have gotten past us!"

The line of soldiers silhouetted against the night sky on the crest of the mountain were no longer flashing their lights, and I was shrouded in darkness. That situation wasn't going to last long; other soldiers were pulling searchlights into positions that would enable them to sweep the entire side of the mountain.

I began inching my way up the edge of the wall on the right side of the platform. I crawled about a hundred feet, then stopped and peered over the edge. Arsenjani was directly below me, commanding the search operation. Mehdi Zahedi had just come down a climbing rope and was bending over the bloody corpse of Darius Khayyam. After a few moments he rose and went to Arsenjani's side.

A soldier emerged from the darkness of the recessed crypt, unzipped his fly and proceeded to urinate on Darius' body. I studied that man very closely; he was tall, walked with a slight limp, and wore an army jacket that was too big for him. He'd become candidate number three.

Arsenjani signaled for the lights to be turned on; it was time to make my selection. Perhaps sensing my presence, Arsenjani suddenly spun around and looked up. What he saw was a very angry dwarf sailing down through the arc of lights at his head.

I was counting on Arsenjani to break my fall; and he did, nicely. Years of circus training had given me the control I needed; I drew my legs in, then snapped my heels forward at the last moment, catching him at the juncture of neck and jaw. I felt his neck snap under the force of the blow, and he was dead before he crumpled to the ground. I landed on top

of him; still, the force of my fall had driven me into Arsenjani hard enough to daze me. I'd hoped to roll up in time to
get a shot at Zahedi; but my brain insisted on seeing everything in pairs, and the air was crowded with bullets.

"*Cease fire!*"

It was Zahedi; apparently he felt it was good politics to
save me for himself. The firing stopped and he came toward
me, his automatic rifle pointed at my chest. I tried to fight
off the dizziness and struggle to my feet, but Zahedi's booted
foot caught me on the side of the head, finishing the job the
fall had started.

18

I CAME OUT OF IT spitting blood on the cold stone. When I
rolled over on my back, my vision slowly cleared; the stars
seemed close enough to touch, like candles that would
flicker out at a wave of my hand. The Big Dipper was directly overhead, and it reminded me of the times when, as a
child, I'd lain in night meadows looking at the stars and
conjuring up other, less cruel worlds where staring at dwarfs
was forbidden. It was all very depressing. More than anything else I wanted to sleep, even if that sleep lasted forever.
Instead, I rolled over onto my stomach, moaning as pain
flashed through my ribs. I quickly took stock. There was a
lot of pain but, miraculously, nothing seemed broken, not
even my head.

Zahedi was standing over me, his lean face pale as death
in the moonlight. Three soldiers kept him company. The rest
of the soldiers were running in and out of the crypt. One
of them had dirt all over his uniform; they'd found the secret tunnel.

"How was it planned for you to leave?" Zahedi's voice was
cold and impatient, just like any New Yorker's.

"Flying carpet," I muttered.

He kicked me expertly, the toe of his boot digging into my shoulder hard enough to cause sufficient agony but not hard enough to break anything. I cursed and tried to maneuver into a position from which I could kick back; I stopped moving when I felt the barrel of a gun against the back of my skull.

Zahedi bent down close to me. "I asked you a question: What was your escape route?"

"Fuck you."

Zahedi gave a curt nod of his head. The gesture infuriated me more than the expected kick. Perhaps it was his youth, his cockiness, his knowledge that he was as much a prodigy in his field as Heifetz and Bobby Fischer had been in theirs. And he had the same awesome self-confidence. Nothing ruffled him; even after all the climbing, he still smelled vaguely of cologne, while I probably stank of fear.

"How did you find us?" I asked.

Zahedi smiled. "I'm afraid you'll have to take the credit for that. It was necessary that we find your body as quickly as possible after you died, not only to cut down on the risk of contagion, but to make sure nobody else found you first and buried your body; that would have made explanations difficult. We sewed a radio direction finder into your clothing. Naturally, Khayyam didn't know that when he picked you up. The direction finder was destroyed when your clothes were burned, but by that time we'd already found the house where they were keeping you. After that it was simply a matter of following the two of you until you led us to something interesting, like the aqueducts of Persepolis." He paused and glanced up to make sure that the soldier behind me had his gun properly placed against my head. "You, Dr. Frederickson, were the Judas goat."

If he expected a reaction, he was disappointed. I was too

tired and hurt to react. Besides, what he said was undoubtedly true. I felt sick.

Zahedi pointed back in the direction of the crypt. "There are guns somewhere in there. We'll find them, you know."

"Sure you will. The trouble is that what you find won't be all there are."

"Then you shall lead us to the rest."

"No, I won't, Zahedi. I can't. They're scattered all over the countryside. You won't know where they are until the shooting starts."

"There's not going to be any shooting." He nodded in the direction of Darius' urine-stained corpse. "The movement is now crushed, leaderless."

"C'mon, kid, you'll never make general with that kind of sloppy thinking. You know as well as I do that Khayyam spent all his time in the United States; he was a planner, not a coordinator. That means there has to be somebody else right here in Iran who's ready to take over. So you just keep looking over your shoulder, Mehdi, m'boy; that person's going to be gunning for you, and I hope to hell he's a good shot. You've got a GEM man in a high position in the SAVAK. It has to be; otherwise, Darius could never have known what was happening to me, much less found me so quickly."

The thin young man looked at me for what seemed a long time. Then he laughed sharply, turned and started to speak to his men in Farsi. It was a long speech, too complicated for me to follow even if I hadn't been punchy. I couldn't understand what he was saying, but I didn't like the reception his speech was getting from the assemblage of soldiers. Their initial response was one of disbelief which rapidly shifted to anger. There were a few muttered curses and much swiveling of heads back and forth between the two bodies on the platform.

I didn't like that, nor did I like it when Zahedi finished his monologue, turned back to me and laughed again. I knew I was going to get a translation I didn't want to hear, but there didn't seem to be much I could do about it; I was the ultimate in captive audiences.

"We've suspected for some time that GEM had infiltrated the SAVAK," Zahedi said easily. "I don't think we have to worry any longer."

"Make your point, you silly son-of-a-bitch. You're not running for office."

"Ah, but I *am*, Frederickson. It's just barely conceivable that this operation could make *me* head of the SAVAK. Besides, I think you already know what I've told my men; I can see it in your face."

"What you see is just good, healthy hatred."

"Arsenjani was your secret ally," he said at last. "*He* was a GEM agent."

"Bullshit," I said with a great deal more certainty than I felt. "Arsenjani poisoned me."

"Sure he did." He spoke loudly, obviously wanting those men who understood English to hear. "And that's how he saved your life: by leaving you out in the desert with nothing more than cholera in you. He knew you'd be found."

"If I'm found with bullets in me, you don't go back to the United States. They don't make young men head of the SAVAK for screw-ups like that."

Zahedi shrugged. "I think you're only half right. I won't be going back to the United States, but that, of course, will be Arsenjani's fault. I'd rather be head of the SAVAK, and if I can convince His Majesty that Arsenjani was a GEM agent, that's exactly what I may become."

"Do I detect a little personal ambition in your patriotic fervor?"

"We've played games long enough," he said, once more speaking to the gallery of soldiers.

Zahedi called out a name and a soldier stepped forward.

He was the tall man with the limp, loose-fitting jacket and weak bladder. Zahedi must have been reading my mind; picking that man as my executioner was the final outrage.

"Shoot him," Zahedi said evenly to the soldier.

My mouth felt as if it were filled with sand, but I still managed to work up some spit, which I deposited on Zahedi's boot. Zahedi casually wiped it off on my sleeve. The guard prodded me to my feet, cocked his rifle and lifted it to his shoulder.

"Not here," Zahedi said in Farsi. He pointed to a stone column at the foot of the mountain, near the edge of the city. "Down below; I'd like him to think about it for a few minutes."

And it would also save them the trouble of carting me down, I thought. Zahedi didn't miss a trick.

The future head of the SAVAK turned and spoke to the rest of the soldiers. Four of them picked up the bodies of Darius and Arsenjani. They carried the corpses to the edge of the platform, then to the right, where stone steps led down to the city. The other soldiers followed. Zahedi spoke a few words to the soldier guarding me; then he too went to the edge of the platform and disappeared into the darkness.

I had no doubt that my executioner was a crack shot, and he was taking no chances. He put down the rifle, looped a rope around my wrists behind me, then took out a pistol, which he stuck into my ear. He pulled on the rope and my hands immediately went numb as the circulation was cut off. The precautions he was taking probably weren't necessary. Sometimes I surprised myself, and I imagined I still had a little fight left in me if I dug deep enough; but for the most part I felt empty, haunted by the specter of Neptune's death —and now Garth's, if he wasn't dead already.

The soldier picked up his rifle again and prodded me in the back. I went to the lip of the platform and down the stone steps. He was good; with one hand holding his rifle and the other holding the rope trailing from my wrists, he never came closer than twenty paces.

I decided the best thing I could hope for was a stab at dying with dignity. It was a hopelessly romantic notion, but I didn't like the idea of groveling before some bastard who was going to piss on me when I was dead.

The soldier dropped the rope when we reached the bottom of the mountain. I walked quickly to the stone column, stood with my back to it and mustered up a wide grin. The soldier stared at me for a few moments with his muddy eyes, then flushed angrily and put his rifle to his shoulder.

The sharp report of a rifle shattered the silence, and my eyes snapped shut. My body quivered in anticipation of steel ripping through my brain; my muscles contracted into a single, tight knot that jackknifed my body forward.

I waited for the pain, the numbness and tearing, the whatever; it didn't come. I waited for a second shot, but still nothing happened. I slowly opened my eyes.

The soldier, still gripping his gun, was slowly sinking to his knees. There was a hole in his forehead the size of a small fist where a dumdum bullet had exited. The bullet had mashed or broken everything inside his head, and his lifeless eyes had turned a bright crimson.

In death, the soldier's finger tightened on the trigger of the automatic rifle and the barrel spewed bullets. The gun barked wildly, the slugs biting into the sand and stone around me and whining off into the darkness. I had some mobility and might have tried to move around to the other side of the column. Instead, I crouched, hugging my knees and trying to make myself as small as possible; I wasn't about to try to outguess the aim of a dead man.

Then the magazine was empty, and the only sound in the city was a persistent ringing in my ears. Finally the soldier toppled over and the gun in his hand clattered on the stone. Now I had time to think of other things, such as the question of who had shot the soldier. And suddenly I knew who it had to be, even before the figure emerged from a cluster of rocks above and made his way quickly down the side of the mountain. I watched him as he reached the base of the mountain and began walking toward me. In the moonlight, Mehdi Zahedi looked even younger than before. But he was certainly a marvel, incredibly fast on his mental toes: for the benefit of the soldiers, he'd done his own little bit of truth-twisting.

He came around behind me, cut the ropes on my wrists, then started to massage my arms. He didn't even glance at the soldier's body. It took me a long time to catch my breath, and when I finally did, I felt as if someone had stolen all the words from my head.

"Shit," I said to loosen up my tongue. "*Damn*, I wish Arsenjani were alive to see you become head of the SAVAK. Did he ever suspect that you were the GEM in his woodpile?"

"Doubtful," Zahedi said tightly. "If he had, I don't think he'd have gone to so much trouble to try to put me back in place in New York. But you never knew with Arsenjani; he was suspicious of everyone. Can you walk?"

"A lot better than I could if your man had shot me. My brother . . . ?"

"Your brother is waiting for you out in the desert with your guide," he said tersely.

"Damn!" I shouted, slapping the stone column. And kept shouting: "*Damn! Damn!*"

"Listen!" Zahedi said, lightly squeezing my arm. "There isn't much time. The SAVAK has had your brother in a hospital, drugged, all this time. He was Arsenjani's ace in the hole in case you couldn't be manipulated. He's been sick. He knows you're going out together, but he doesn't know that he's a walking warehouse filled with SAVAK lies. He's still weak and dopey. You'll have to straighten him out."

"Oh, Christ, *I'll* straighten him out," I said, feeling more than a bit dopey with hysteria myself. "How did you rescue him?"

He shook his head impatiently. "There's no time to explain now. Suffice it to say that Arsenjani will get the blame. But we have to hurry. My men should have gone by now, but the shooting could bring them back."

Zahedi started to move off into the shadows on my right. I moved out after him and promptly fell on my face; my legs were vibrating like tuning forks. Zahedi came back and helped me to my feet. I did better the second time. We moved off to the right a hundred yards, then headed back toward the mountain. There were no sounds of pursuit.

We reached the edge of the dead city and Zahedi pointed to a piece of broken column on the ground. "Rest," he said. "I think we're safe for the moment."

The muscles in my legs had stopped their spasms, but now it was my head that was shaking. Giddy with relief, I was hungry for the truth—all of it. "*You*," I said. "Everything you said about Arsenjani applies to you. You're the key to this whole thing."

He shook his head. "I'm just one member of a team of men trying to do what we know is right for our country before Pahlavi destroys it."

"Your father has to be GEM's operational head in Iran, right?"

"Yes," he said, quickly glancing around him. "I suppose you may as well know all of it. He and Darius began planning this many years ago."

"But why should your *father*—" I broke off in mid-sentence; it isn't polite to question the motives of the father of the man who's just saved your life.

Mehdi smiled wryly. "It's true that my father is a very rich man; but even rich men sometimes have ideals. My father has *always* known that he's a member of a very small minority. He loves our land and its people. He believes in Iran, and he believes that it can again be great—but only with a representative government. He's one of the men who originally took from the land—as was Darius. Now my father is paying his debt. In short, my father believes in freedom and he taught me his lesson well."

"*You* didn't know about the bug in my clothing."

"That's right," he said thickly. "My ignorance cost Darius his life."

Now things were dropping into place like tumblers in a combination lock. The pieces of the puzzle were finally coming together, in living color and right side up. I whistled softly, admiringly. "If I can still count right, you come out a triple agent. Ali and the members of the Confederation think you're a student leader, the SAVAK thinks you're one of them, while the bottom line is that you're GEM. Obviously, you didn't *want* to go back to the United States. You made sure you left a clear trail when you flew out, and it was *Darius* who tipped John Simpson on how to pick it up."

"Yes. We gambled on the possibility that Ali would hire a private detective if I didn't return, so I left a letterhead and a plastic business card from Bannon's company where a good investigator, working from an anonymous tip, could find them. There was also a note which looked like a reminder I'd written to myself about the plane reservation. As you've guessed, we wanted my role as a SAVAK agent to be exposed."

I thought about the letterhead and note. The papers that had led Simpson to Orrin Bannon's operation—and brought Hassan Khordad down on his head—would have been destroyed by the water in the East River. "Then the whole idea from the beginning was to discredit you with the Confederation of Iranian Students so that you'd be *forced* to stay here. The problem was that Simpson was killed before he could tell Ali what he'd found out."

Zahedi nodded. "It looked as though I'd have to go back."

"Oh-oh. This sounds like where I came along."

"Right. But there's no more time to talk. You have to go now. It's almost dawn, and the desert will be hot."

I didn't move. I was too close to all the answers to be in a hurry. "How long do you think your cover as a SAVAK agent is going to last?"

"Indefinitely—assuming your cooperation. But a few weeks is all I need. Then the time for secrets will be past; the real fighting will begin."

"How did you fake cholera?"

He laughed tightly, and I thought I saw him shudder. "There's no way to fake cholera: I contracted it purposely. It was a gamble, but I was reasonably sure I'd live. We needed the time; I had to find a way to delay my return to the university. Firouz Maleki, as you know, occupied a very high post in our command structure. When he was captured we knew that the planning phase was over, and that my place was in Iran."

"And, of course, the SAVAK wanted to send you back to the United States because they assumed that was where the leadership was."

"Yes. With the private detective dead, Arsenjani considered it safe for me to return with some kind of cover story; he was quite insistent." He paused, smiled. "Then you indeed came along. In a way, you represented GEM's last hope for keeping me in Iran as a member of the army and the SAVAK. It was obvious that I couldn't go back while there was even a possibility that you'd linked me to the SAVAK, and I argued—quite correctly, as it turned out—that you'd made such a connection when you killed Khordad. Then Arsenjani came up with the plan of luring you here and convincing you that Khordad, Bannon *and* I were GEM." He frowned slightly, scratched his arm. "Frankly, I

225

was surprised by his persistence in such a complicated plan. Now I believe he wanted something else from you."

"You heard him ask about a list of SAVAK agents. What was that all about?"

He shrugged. "I don't know. As I've told you, Arsenjani was extremely devious and trusted no one." He paused, thought about it, let it go. "I understand the royal idiot spoke to you personally."

"Yeah. He had a simple solution to the whole problem; he wanted to buy me."

"You came down on the right side, Dr. Frederickson."

"It's your war, not mine, Mehdi," I said quietly. "I just couldn't stand the thought of all that financial security. Who ever heard of a rich dwarf? People wouldn't take me seriously."

He smiled thinly. "I think I understand."

"That was some improvisation you did up there on the mountain. And I think I know what it cost you. Unless dumdum bullets are standard army issue, I think I know how you felt when Darius was killed."

Zahedi said nothing. I hauled myself to my feet with a groan. I was still wobbly, but I knew I was going to make it. I didn't know whether Garth could yet forgive me for Neptune's death; but at least he was alive, and that was enough to put life into my legs.

"You killed Maleki when you came to interrogate him, didn't you?" I asked, looking up at the mountain.

When he didn't answer, I looked back at him; he seemed years older. He slowly nodded. "Firouz held out until I arrived. Shortly after that, I managed . . . to help him commit suicide." His voice cracked, and he cleared his throat. "He knew the risks from the beginning. When the time came, he was willing to pay the price of his commitment."

"You fellows play a rough game, Mehdi."

"There's a lot at stake."

"And a tricky one, if you'll allow an understatement."

"We've had centuries of practice," he said wryly.

"Ali Azad really doesn't know anything at all about this, does he?"

"No, and I can assure you that I'll be a dead man if he finds out what I'm really doing. He *must* believe that I am what you thought me to be up until a few minutes ago—a SAVAK agent."

"Ali is an *informer*?"

"Ali isn't, but almost a quarter of the membership of the Confederation is, including the girl, Anna. That's why it was so easy for the SAVAK and U.S. Military Intelligence to keep track of what you were doing and thinking."

"That surprises me," I said, thinking of the beautiful, doe-eyed girl in the C.I.S. office.

He shrugged. "Anna considers herself a patriot. In any case, Ali does have a tendency to talk too much; he talks to Anna, and she talks to the SAVAK. I'm asking you to help me carry out this charade because my life depends on it. I won't ask you to give me a yes or no answer. You know the facts, and you've seen a part of what it is we're trying to change."

"I'll keep your secret," I said quietly. "You wouldn't have saved my life if you thought otherwise. How are you going to explain the dead soldier?"

"Another one of Arsenjani's mistakes, and all the more reason to place me at the head of the SAVAK."

"Good luck, Mehdi," I said, starting to walk away. My legs felt like rubber, but they held me up; now all they had to do was carry me two miles.

"Professor Frederickson!" Zahedi called after me. "I'm sorry I don't have any water to give you."

I stopped, turned. "Don't worry about it," I called back.

"Your *nom de guerre* is Mehdi Zahedi; mine's Camel."

"You're hurt, and you don't have a compass. Can you make it?"

When I looked up at the sky, I found my childhood friends still there; the brilliant North Star would guide me on the way to the end of the first leg of my journey home. It would be there for another half hour or so; after that I would have the sun, then Garth and our guide.

"Hey, ever since I was turned down by the Boy Scouts as a kid I've always made it a point to know what direction I'm traveling in. I'll make it to the camels; I'm more concerned about making it *on* my camel."

"I hope we'll meet again in better times."

I turned and headed up the side of the mountain.

19

HE CAME AT ME from the east, out of the sun—a tall, most un-Arab-looking figure bouncing up and down on his camel like a yo-yo. He saw me running toward him and dug his heels into the beast, which promptly braked to a stop, hurling him over its head onto the sand. A moment later I was on him, pounding his chest, rolling around with him until we were both too exhausted to move.

"You're a few hours late, brother," Garth wheezed.

"Shit. *You're* no one to talk about being late."

"I knew you were going to make it! I *told* her no one was going to kill my brother!"

I sat up. "You told whom?"

Garth rolled over onto his side and propped himself up on his elbow. He was thin and pale, eyes too bright, but I couldn't remember ever seeing him look so happy. "*Neptune!*" he shouted. "Can you *believe* it? She's alive, and she's *here!*"

"Where is she?"

"We split up to look for you."

"Where's our guide?"

"Hey, this is no time to talk about it," Garth said, starting to rise. "Let's get out of here. We'll hit a few East Side bars, get drunk for a week and swap stories. To tell you the truth, I'm a little tired of Iran."

I grabbed his shirt collar and pulled him back down to the ground. Behind him, over his shoulder, I could see a lone rider coming up on us, and I didn't want Garth to know. "Let's talk about it now. Where's our guide?"

He looked at me strangely, then shrugged. "He never showed up."

Instinctively I glanced back in the direction of Persepolis; I imagined I could hear a soft wind filled with ancient voices blowing from it. "But Neptune did."

The figure on the camel had seen us and was now coming up fast. Garth still hadn't noticed. He was sitting up now, holding his head. "I'm still so damned . . . light-headed. I picked up one hell of a bug as soon as I got here. I remember . . . being taken to a hospital, out of my head with fever. And that's the *last* I remember until a . . . few days ago when I came out of it. Neptune was there with me."

"Harry Stans told me you got a message from her family inviting you to come here for her funeral."

He shook his head. "I misunderstood. They don't write English that well. She'd been tortured very badly, then *left* for dead. But somebody found her, and her family had her flown back here for treatment. It wasn't until she'd recovered that she could tell them about me, and by then I was already here—in the hospital."

"*Hello*, Precious!" Neptune cried as she came up on her camel, stopped beside us. An expert rider, she sat easily in the saddle. She was wearing an Arab burnoose as protection against the desert heat; her face and its lovely crown of black-and-silver hair were hidden beneath its hood. In the shadow of the garment her eyes shone like twin moons. I wasn't surprised when she didn't dismount.

"Hello, Neptune," I said easily. "Surprised to see me?"

"Surprised? Precious, I'm *delighted* to see you."

I strolled casually to where I'd dropped the automatic rifle Mehdi had given me. I picked it up, brought it back and firmly placed it in a bewildered Garth's hands. Then I quickly stepped behind Neptune's camel and anchored myself in position by gripping the animal's tail.

"Lady, you call me 'precious' one more time and I'll pull your fucking camel out from under you."

"*Mongo*—"

"What the hell's the matter with you?" Garth growled, leaping to his feet. "You're talking to Neptune!"

"Your lady's SAVAK, Garth," I said. "One of the Chief Honcho's private stock; she's probably a relative."

"You're out of your head, brother," Garth said menacingly. "You're talking about the woman I'm going to marry, and I want you to shut your mouth *now!*"

Neptune said nothing. Her camel turned and I moved with it, keeping low under its rump and hoping it wouldn't decide to start kicking. "The SAVAK put you in the hospital!" I shouted at Garth as I spat dust out of my mouth. "You were supposed to take my place as the bearer of tall tales, and incidentally—as I see it now—used to put a second top agent back into place. By the way, Neptune: Arsenjani's dead. Sorry to have to break the news to you in such a harsh way."

"Mongo!" she cried. "*Stop* this foolishness! I want to help you get *away* from here!"

"Oh, I'll *bet* you do, sweetheart. What you really want is to find out how I happen to be here in the first place. You're not going to find out."

"*Mongo*—"

Garth started walking unsteadily toward me; I released one hand and pointed at him. "Garth, this is Mongo talking. You've known me a hell of a lot longer than Neptune, and

231

the least you owe me is a good listen. Get your head clear; there's a lot you don't know, and you're going to have to start putting it together fast if we're going to get out of here alive. Now, this lady has a gun under her saddle blankets, so you'd damn well better get back to yours. You're going to have to decide what to do with it."

"If Neptune's SAVAK," Garth growled, "why didn't she just shoot us both when she rode up?"

"Because she knows it had to be a GEM agent who helped me escape, and it's her job to find out who it was. And coming out with you—with us—was still the smartest way for her to return to the United States. After all, if a question ever came up concerning her apparent death and resurrection, *you'd* be there to supply the answers. She was hoping she could *still* pull it off, even with me around. Now she knows it won't work, and you'd damn well better believe that all she's doing now is waiting for the right instant. If this camel kicks my ass, or you blink the wrong way, we're dead men."

Garth and I looked at each other a long time before he slowly turned around and went back to the rifle he'd left on the sand. He didn't pick it up . . . but he stayed close.

"*Garth!*" Neptune gasped.

"Keep talking, Mongo," Garth said breathlessly. "And talk fast. If I don't like what you have to say, we part company—here."

The camel moved again, quickly and sharply, this time in response to Neptune's tug on the reins. I was pulled off my feet, but I managed to hang on to the tail and come up again while at the same time staying clear of the sharp hooves. "She had plenty of time to get out of Bannon's building!" I shouted, gagging on the dust that had been thrown up. "I should have realized it at the time, but I was out of my head with guilt. Remember how interested she was in this case right from the beginning? Remember how much she wanted to help? Goddamn *right* she wanted to help, because she had a vital interest in finding out what was going on! She hung around the building after I told her to leave, then identified herself as a SAVAK agent to Khordad when he showed up! She had to find out what I knew and what I was up to!"

"Garth," Neptune sighed, "I *love* you."

"I met Neptune *weeks* before you got on the case," Garth said in a hoarse, agonized voice. 'How could she have been connected with it?"

"She *wasn't* connected, brother. Not then. At that time she was using *you*. She said it once in joking, but it was the truth; she knew that a simple burglary like the one she'd had in her apartment wasn't going to get all that much attention from the N.Y.P.D., not unless she made certain someone took a special interest in the case. That's why she made a play for the investigating detective—*you*, Garth."

Another sharp swerve; I managed to hang on. "Remember the papers I found in Khordad's trunk?" I continued through clenched teeth. "Well, the SAVAK is really into false bottoms. Neptune didn't care about her jewelry; it was the jewelry *box* she wanted back. She was one of Arsenjani's supervisors. She was working on the GEM business independently, while at the same time checking on the SAVAK agents in the United States; Arsenjani was a sneaky bastard. Neptune actually had a *list* of those agents in a false bottom in her jewelry box. She couldn't make another move until she found out *who* had taken it—a common burglar, which she could have lived with, or GEM agents, which would be a catastrophe. *That* was when she latched on to you."

For the first time, Garth spoke directly to the woman he loved. "Neptune, you *were* interested in the box more than anything else."

"It was an heirloom, Garth," she said tightly. "I explained that to you."

"She was scared!" I shouted. "With the loss of that list it

was *her* head on the block until she got it back—or determined that it hadn't been stolen by GEM agents who were on to her! It *really* made her nervous when Zahedi dropped out of sight, because his name was on that list. Then all hell started breaking loose. She didn't know what was going on. Then *I* came onto the scene and she figured she could find out through me."

"If Neptune and Zahedi are both SAVAK," Garth said tensely, "she'd have *known* why Zahedi left."

"Uh-uh. She was cut off. She'd cut *herself* off after losing the list. She couldn't very well contact Arsenjani and ask him for information without admitting she'd made a very bad mistake."

"Why would she fake her own death?"

"She'd played out her string, Garth. By that time she knew she had to go back and face Arsenjani no matter *who* had engineered the burglary. Besides, she assumed I was a dead man, and that posed a big risk. I'd picked her up at her apartment; a beautiful woman with a dwarf isn't that common a sight to begin with, not even in New York—and people do know me. She was afraid that sooner or later you might connect us on that day, and she figured it was best to simply go back to Iran and regroup. By last week, with my death imminent and no other SAVAK agents blown, Arsenjani figured it was safe to put *her* back in place, with you as the vehicle. Garth, I'm betting that having GEM spring you was as big a surprise to *her* as it was to you; I'm betting that *you* contacted *her* after the arrangements were made. Am I right?"

"It's true," Garth said in a voice I could barely hear above the snorts of Neptune's camel.

"You told her about the guide, and she just had time to take him out before the two of you took off."

Neptune had heard enough. She made the move I'd been expecting, but there was very little I could do about it. As she reached for the rifle under her saddle blankets, I tugged sharply on the camel's tail. The animal bucked and kicked, knocking me onto my back on the warming sand. She managed to get off a burst of fire at Garth, but the movement of her mount made it impossible for her to aim. For one horrible moment I thought he was just going to stand there and let Neptune kill him; but he finally picked up the rifle, aimed carefully and killed her with a single round. She fell next to me in a bloody, lifeless heap.

"*Garth*," I said, rising to my knees as he staggered toward me. "I—"

"Shut up," he said.

Weeping, he picked up Neptune's body and carried her thirty paces away. There he set her down and proceeded to dig a grave in the sand with his hands. That accomplished, he gently laid the body in the grave and covered it over. Then he sat down next to the grave, crossed his legs Indian style and bowed his head. I hunched down on the sand twenty yards behind him and waited.

Two hours later he stood, wiped his eyes, turned and walked back toward me. I rose and waited for him. He stopped a few paces away, looked into my eyes and smiled thinly.

"You looked funny as hell holding on to that camel's tail, you know. Very undignified."

"I'll bet," I said in a whisper.

"What would you have done if he crapped on you?"

"Surrender immediately, of course. I believe in omens."

"I love you, brother."

"And I love you, Garth."

"Do you suppose this is what they mean by 'male bonding'?"

"I think so. In the movie, you'll be played by Robert Redford. I get John Wayne."

"Got it," he said. "Now, do you suppose Mom and Pop

Frederickson's two boys can find their way out of this giant sandbox?"

"There's not a doubt in my mind."

"How will we find our contacts?"

"We'll let them find us. We'll just truck up and down the Gulf on our trusty steeds. Have you ever seen any dwarf sheikhs?"

Garth indicated the camels. "Which one do you want?"

"Yours. You can have the one with the sore ass; he keeps looking at me in an odd way."

We got onto the camels and rode into the blazing afternoon. Garth looked back only once at the small mound we'd left behind.

He's rough, he's tough, he's "everything a hero ought to be."

—St. Louis Post-Dispatch

He's detective Harry Stoner. And this time he's taking on the seedy world of drug suppliers and unscrupulous football coaches to find out who destroyed an all-pro noseguard named Billy Parks and created a monster whose only reality was winning the game in...

LIFE'S WORK
A Harry Stoner Mystery
by Jonathan Valin
14790-5 $3.50

"Valin's '80's equivalent of Chandler's Philip Marlowe and McDonald's Lew Archer is a craggy, competent and complex private eye named Harry Stoner, whose fan club of readers and critics is increasing with each caper."—Los Angeles Times

Watch for more Harry Stoner Mysteries... coming soon to bookstores near you!

At your local bookstore or use this handy coupon for ordering:

**DELL READERS SERVICE, DEPT. DJV
P.O. Box 5057, Des Plaines, IL. 60017-5057**

Please send me the above title(s). I am enclosing $_____. (Please add $1.50 per order to cover shipping and handling.) Send check or money order—no cash or C.O.D.s please.

Ms./Mrs./Mr. _____

Address _____

City/State_____ Zip _____

DJV-1/88

Prices and availability subject to change without notice. Please allow four to six weeks for delivery. This offer expires 7/88.

Match wits with the best-selling
MYSTERY WRITERS
in the business!

ROBERT BARNARD
"A new grandmaster."—*The New York Times*
___CORPSE IN A GILDED GAGE   11465-9 $3.50
___OUT OF THE BLACKOUT   16761-2 $3.50

SIMON BRETT
"He's bloody marvelous!"—*Chicago Sun Times*
___DEAD GIVEAWAY   11914-6 $3.50
___SHOCK TO THE SYSTEM   18200-X $3.50

MARTHA GRIMES
"A writer to relish."—*The New Yorker*
___THE DIRTY DUCK   12050-0 $3.50
___I AM THE ONLY RUNNING
    FOOTMAN   13924-4 $3.95

SISTER CAROL ANNE O'MARIE
"Move over Miss Marple..."—*San Francisco Sunday Examiner & Chronicle*
___A NOVENA FOR MURDER   16469-9 $3.25

JONATHAN VALIN
"A superior writer...smart and sophisticated."
      —*The New York Times Book Review*
___LIFE'S WORK   14790-5 $3.50

A SPENSER NOVEL

Robert B. PARKER

"The toughest, funniest, wisest private-eye in the field."*

☐ TAMING A SEA-HORSE	18841-5	$4.50
☐ A CATSKILL EAGLE	11132-3	$3.95
☐ VALEDICTION	19246-3	$3.95
☐ THE WIDENING GYRE	19535-7	$3.95
☐ CEREMONY	10993-0	$3.95
☐ A SAVAGE PLACE	18095-3	$3.95
☐ EARLY AUTUMN	12214-7	$3.95
☐ LOOKING FOR RACHEL WALLACE	15316-6	$3.95
☐ THE JUDAS GOAT	14196-6	$3.95
☐ PROMISED LAND	17197-0	$3.95
☐ MORTAL STAKES	15758-7	$3.95
☐ GOD SAVE THE CHILD	12899-4	$3.95
☐ THE GODWULF MANUSCRIPT	12961-3	$3.95

*The Houston Post

 At your local bookstore or use this handy coupon for ordering:

DELL READERS SERVICE, DEPT. DRP
P.O. Box 5057, Des Plaines, IL. 60017-5057

Please send me the above title(s). I am enclosing $_____. (Please add $1.50 per order to cover shipping and handling.) Send check or money order—no cash or C.O.D.s please.

Ms./Mrs./Mr. _____

Address _____

City/State _____ Zip _____

DRP-1/88

Prices and availability subject to change without notice. Please allow four to six weeks for delivery. This offer expires 7/88.